# ENERGY IN VAIN

AKSHAT SRESHTIN

First Published in June 2023

**ISBN: 978-93-5819-480-7**

**BLUEROSE PUBLISHERS**

www.BlueRoseONE.com

info@bluerosepublishers.com

+91 8882 898 898

**Cover Design:**

Yash

**Typographic Design:**

Pooja Sharma

**Distributed by:** BlueRose, Amazon, Flipkart

# Dedication

DEDICATED TO MY SCHOOL

'MANJUSRI PUBLIC SCHOOL, SIKKIM'

# Think Again!

What do you think
        is the sum of freedom?
What do you think
        is the subtraction of distraction?

What do you think is divide
        of someone who lied?
What do you think is multiply
        of someone who is shy?

How do you think to burry
        destruction caused by worry?
How do you think to be fool
        when someone is breaking the rule?

How can you think not to borrow

when your friend is sorrow?

Why can you not be satisfied

with whatever you have side?

Please don't dig a mine

to destroy the land which is fine.

Be like the Sun which comes everyday

even though, it is Sunday.

Don't be the one

who gives tough-time memory.

You should have fun

as time is on run.

Don't make things a habit

or else it will be a trend.

Don't say things which our mind grabs it

or else you will take time to mend it.

Akshat Sreshtin

# Acknowledgment

I would like to thank my school for giving me such an environment to write books and poems.

I am also thankful to my friends especially Kyorzang Bhutia, who provided me immense support by providing me his genuine feedback.

I would like to thank everyone who devoted to edit and publish this book.

And special thanks to my father for being a Beta Reader, Development editor and Chief editor.

***Thank you***

***for making a piece of story into a book!***

Hope you will like this book!

**Akshat Sreshtin**

**3rd June, 2023**

akshatsreshtin@gmail.com

# Contents

# 1.

# Unique Energy

'Hellry wake up' said his father excitedly, 'Today is your test', he continued. This sentence hit his head like a fastball striking a cricketer's bat and with a milder swing goes off the boundary with everyone leaving awful.

With such quick and vigour, he jumped from his bed. Done his morning chores in very haste while his mind was running like a wild horse, thinking, revising, solving, and a lot more. Suddenly, he said in astonishment, 'Oh, NO...' and moved as fast as he can, to his reading shelf. And from the stacked books, notes, and magazines, he searched for a small sheet of paper with mumbling something in quick succession and moving his eyes and fingers at the same pace as both were fixed. He stopped his fingers but his eyes moved a little further. He has to draw his eyes back to that position and look suspiciously. When he ascertained himself then he slowly moved that pile of books and cautiously took it out.

He was still mumbling and going through all words and sentences paying extra attention to formulas and keywords. He was taken aback by something. He made some changes and attached an extra sheet of paper as a special note. And kept everything in his odd-looking purple coloured bag which was not only designed by him but also sewn by himself in his Craft classes. He headed for his school, as always in a haste.

When he reached school, everything in himself started changing in him.

Nervousness and confusion took over his vigour and astonishment, letting him forget many things, if not everything.

He took out his sheets of paper and now he was gazing through it as if it was not his.

He shivered with fright because of the 'Thud' of the door. When he looked towards the door, he calmed himself as it was his science teacher. While he was collecting himself, a loud voice filled with the energies of his science teacher again distracted him. 'Good morning class' said his teacher excitedly. She added, 'Are you all ready for the test'.

'Let me explain to you about today's test' that I told you earlier also that today there will be a chemistry test in which you have to use chemicals and the properties of different foodstuffs to find the nutritive value of food.

With these instructions, they were asked to go to the chemistry laboratory where they were asked to move to their allotted positions. At every stand, they have their chemicals, beakers, flasks, spirit lamp, and other necessary stuff alongwith the required chemicals with many other chemicals as well as they were given a sheet of instructions on Do's and Don'ts of chemical laboratory.

The teacher announced, 'Class! All the best! Now you may proceed with the experiments.'

Till now, he was nervous and confused but now a feeling of jealousy added, as his brother, who is just senior to him by some minutes as both are twins, got a simpler one according to Hellry's perception. Hellry was completely blank.

He mixed the wrong chemicals leading to a violent reaction like an explosion but it was not an explosion. There were flashes of light.

Hellry felt down. Everyone including the teacher and laboratory gathered around Hellry. He was lying on the ground- silent and composed. Students thought that something very bad had happened to Hellry, some even thought that he abode them for another world. But no one was trying to touch him because a very special light or fume or something else appears to radiate from his body. Either they were mystified or frightened or anxious, it is tough to say.

However, one of the laboratory staff who was outside the laboratory to collect additional sheets from the store, came and seeing the people gathered at a point, went straight to that place, cleared his passage to the center, and saw a boy lying down. He swung in action and does not wait for anything or called anyone. But directly leaned to him and carried him in his arms and rushed towards the door. Finding the revolving office chair, he tied Hellry lightly to the office chair with the help of teachers and other laboratory staff, who have now recollected themselves, and moved him directly to the school infirmary.

Where the doctor examined him and checked his vitals- ABC (Airway, Breathing, and Circulation). His vitals were very normal, but he was unconscious. The doctor without taking any extra minutes referred him to a higher centre. The school vehicle moved him to the nearest medical college where again a team of doctors alongwith students and juniors checked his vitals as well as many more signs and symptoms. But were taken aback when they found that all the vitals are very normal but had a very poor scale on Glasgow Coma Scale. They thought that Hellry's brain stopped working, which means he is brain-dead.

But before taking any final decision they thought to have an MRI of his brain. Meanwhile, their parents accompanied by his brother and class teacher arrived at the hospital. All were worried as well as anxious to know about the problem which his son Hellry was suffering from. Soon they got the MRI report which was revealing everything normal. There was no sign of concussion or contusion, no internal haemorrhage, or anything significant. Doctors were perplexed, which added anxiousness to teachers and parents.

Soon teacher narrated the whole episode to the doctors. Listening to the teacher, doctors decided to make a team of senior doctors, physicists, and chemists from the varied field doing research.

Within a few hours, all team members united in a very large hall where Hellry was brought alongwith his teacher and parents. They requested the teacher to explain every minute detail about the incident, better to say accident, as who knows whether it was an incident or an accident.

The teacher informed them about the chemistry laboratory test about ascertaining the nutritive value and type of nutritional content in a different type of food. The teacher also explained, 'How Hellry mixed the wrong chemicals leading to this fatal episode.' The team also became anxious to know about the afterward things that ensued.

The teacher recalled looking upward and told, 'It was as if something was coming out from the Hellry, say a light, but it was not light as we see, or an energy which was glowing him. But there is general warmness with light, however, there is a feeling of coldness or pleasing feel with that light-like thing.

On this account, the Team showed their interest to visit the school. Thus, they departed for school. However, they were saddened upon reaching the school because all the mess was cleaned thoroughly and the laboratory was appearing very neat and clean as if nothing has happened in the morning.

While they were thinking about how to ascertain what has been mixed and what has formed and what had happened, one of the team- member's phone ranged. For receiving the call, he moved a little away from the team.

Others were talking about the possible happening. They were interrupted by the first one who left them to attend the call. He was excited and ordered everyone to move towards the car as they have to rush to the centre. He was in such haste that no one thought of even asking what has happened. All rushed. There was a pin drop of silence in the car. Everyone was engulfed by thought which was ranging from nowhere to everywhere.

Perceiving the seriousness of the matter and time, the driver flew the car while considering the traffic and norms of the road and reached the centre as fast as he can drive. As the driver stopped the car with a sudden break, it appears that the break has also been applied to the ranging thoughts of team members. Everyone looked toward the one who received the call. He by moving his eyes directed everyone to follow him.

All jumped out of the car and followed him and in a matter of seconds, they realized that they are heading towards the hall where Hellry was kept.

When they reached the hall, their eyes freeze in astonishment. They stopped moving. It appears that they became a statue in the game of 'statue and go'.

They were greeted by no one other than Hellry himself that too in a clear voice as if nothing has happened. One scientist, with anxiousness, asked, 'Are you ....' But interrupted by Hellry's father in excitement, 'Can we take him home as he is now fine.'

Everyone looked towards each other and nodded in 'yes'.

# 2.
# Visit

Almost a month has passed, Hellry has resumed his normal activity. His father and mother always instruct Hellry to be extra cautious and they were giving extra attention to Hellry. As they too wanted to do so, like any other parent, but they were instructed by that team also to keep a vigil on his activities, mood, food habits, extra, extra, almost everything.

His brother, who was very rational and scientific in approach and always use to scan himself to do any changes in his thought or modify his lifestyle so that he should be empathetic even to his enemies and make this world a sustainable place, was obviously trying to help Hellry.

Hellry initially enjoyed this extra attention as he has had a serious complaint since his childhood that he did not receive much love and affection not only from his parent but also from anyone in society or school because of Heven as he used to be very nice to everyone. Which according to Hellry, his brother, Heven, do it to show off and insult him.

Later Hellry realized that with extra attention, comes a lot of new things like responsibility. So, he started feeling suffocated. He asked his father, 'I wanted to visit my grandparents.' Since his father was also receiving a lot of calls from his parents about the well-being of Hellry. Hellry's father decided to take a break.

Soon Hellry and Heven packed their stuff and departed to meet their grandparents after a gap of about five years. They were accompanied by their parent. When they were about to reach, his father asked her mother to drive. Hellry and Heven were surprised listening to this because they all know that driving is the passion of their father, that too, a long drive, and in the woods. His father took them here and there just to drive the car. Even they visited about four hundred kilometres, took rest in a motel, and returned back, just to enjoy driving. This is the most interesting road trip that they are witnessing right now as there is lush greenery with no traffic and pollution. It seems that the road has been built for them only.

Although mother moved to the driving seat but she was continuously looking towards father as to ask something or pacify him. They were a bit confused as they have never seen their father behaving like this and preventing eye contact with anyone.

Anyhow they reached to an ancient-looking building with no gates in front and no marks of a road inside the boundary. They, crushing the grasses and small flowered Tulips, reached the portico where his grandparent received Hellry and Heven by kissing and hugging and trying to look straight into the eyes of their father. But again, he was keeping himself away from looking in the eyes, trying to look here and there.

As father was looking here and there which let Hellry and Heven also to look the surrounding. Soon they saw something which made them astonished and they freed themselves from the clutches of their grandparents and ran towards the path through which they travelled inside the boundary. Hellry for the first time gazed towards Heven, and it seemed that he was asking 'How.' Heven sat on his knees and in order to confirm his sight he touched the grasses and flowered Tulips which were crushed by the tyres. It appears that nothing has passed through that garden.

Their grandfather walked towards them and asked them to follow. Though his voice was very feeble and gentle, but it was much like commanding. So, both followed behind them. While walking Hellry tried to hold his grandfather's hand. As he touched his grandfather's hand, his grandfather stopped for a moment and looked straight into the eyes of Hellry with astonishment, soon he gathered himself and moved forward.

They all gathered at the dining table which was mesmerizing although it was made up of jungle woods and have no painting or design. But it seems that the dining table was greeting them every now and then. They enjoyed the sumptuous food. But one thing still hounding both Hellry and Heven that they were seeing his father so quiet for the first time. He was not even so quiet or serious when he became jobless for about eleven months because of the end of the contract period and there was grave concern for money.

After lunch and about a solar day-long journey they were very tired and they took permission to take a rest. All left for their respective rooms as shown and directed by her grandmother.

About an hour passed, Hellry felt that someone is sitting beside him. He looked and found his grandfather was near him. Hellry was thinking that what to say. Meanwhile, his grandfather exclaimed, 'I was guessing right that you ....' 'Guessing what', Hellry interrupted. ‘Okay, it means that you still do not know about all this. ‘About what’, he loudly asked with surprises running in his veins. He was chilled.

‘Okay let me speak’, feebly said his grandfather. Hellry became much more attentive and like a good listener made direct eye contact with his grandfather, which was tough to do as there is great depth in his eyes. However, Hellry was determined to listen with full attention so he was keeping good eye contact.

‘Listen Hellry, what I suspect that you have got that purple sheet’, inquired his grandpa.

Hellry made a great deal of effort in recalling and arranging the fact that which purple sheets were talked about. Nonetheless, Hellry was thinking. His grandfather added, 'Related to the nutritive value of food.' This was the biggest hint that he received as the whole thing started with this. 'Yes, I got that almost a year ago while cleaning the drawer of that old table which was given to me at that time when dad was facing a financial crisis so he took it out from the storeroom and mended himself and handed it to me.'

'I was quite fascinated by that purple sheet as it talks about the elements, that too only four main elements- Carbon, Hydrogen, Oxygen, and Nitrogen, and their role in energy transfer.' He continued, 'Since I know that I will get a freehand in the chemistry exam as there will be all chemicals...' His grandparent asked hastily, his calmness broke and the depth of his eyes gone, 'Where is the paper? Have you followed it from first to last? Have you tweaked it?'

Tell me, Hellry everything. Recall it properly. I have dedicated my whole life to it. This is the cause of concern between your father and me. I ... I have never been able to give him much time when he was a child. How has he grown up? What was his concern? Gone missing from my life. I can't reverse it. When he has grown up. I always insisted him to take my work and carry my experiments further. He denied. He denied it completely. He ..... .The eyes of Hellry's grandfather filled up. He was very emotional. On the verge of crying. However, it was tough to say whether he was emotional because of guilt or the denial of my father.

Soon, his grandfather returned back to normalcy and again started inquiring about the same where he left.

Now Hellry started narrating about the episode. But there was nothing that excited his grandfather, although he felt very painful when he learned that Hellry has lost that purple sheet in that accident.

However, he again asked him to recall. He enquired, 'Have you mixed everything in right proportion.'

Hellry thought and then replied, 'As that day was a chemistry test and I was prepared to do my chemical reaction as shown in the purple sheet. So, I was a bit confused and nervous as those were not taught in my class nor I found it on the internet when I searched for the same.' 'I did the same as per my sheet, as I want to be perfect' He added.

Grandfather corrected, 'Not as per your sheet, but according to that purple sheet.'

Hellry, 'NO.. Not Grandpa. It was as per my sheet, not purple sheet because I have made certain last-time changes that morning which I felt while doing my morning chores.'

'What changes? Hellry!'

'Be at point! Tell me! What changes you have made!'

'Sorry, Grandpa. It was tough to recall. As a thought honked in my mind. I corrected in that purple sheet. Since I was getting late that morning. And later you all know about that incident. Sorry.. accident.'

'Leave it. Tell me another thing what you know or your friends, brother, teacher, or parent have told you about you just after that episode.' Hellry bounced back jokingly, 'Yes. They told me a light-like thing was coming out of me which was very pleasing. But it was not li......'

'Yes. Yes. Yes. It had worked' his grandpa jumped excitedly and said in excitement while interrupting Hellry. You come with me. Fast. Be fast Hellry.

# 3.

# Realization

Hellry jumped from his bed and followed his grandpa towards a narrow lane adjacent to the garden and house. Soon his grandpa cleared the web cobs on the old-looking door which seemed to have not been opened in the last four to five years. And opened the door. Hellry was astonished to see inside. It was a complete laboratory as large as his school football ground. There was everything that Hellry has either seen in the school laboratory or in any sci-fi movies.

But his grandpa went towards a machine looking like a dentist's chair and asked Hellry to sit on it.

Hellry with a feeble voice enquired, 'Grandpa! Will you do experiments with me as villains do in sci-fi movies?'

'No. No Hellry. It is just to check what powers have you gained.'

No power grandpa. I have no power. As if nothing has happened to me. I am very normal like before.

Don't be awful or anxious. Seat calmly. Let me record all the things. He turned on all the cameras of that lab.

As the machine started whirling and booting and a lot of different types of sound filled the lab, making Hellry very uncomfortable. His grandpa in order to allay his fear introduced himself and his profession. He told him, "I was a gold medallist in Physics and Chemistry. He continued, "But when I become Diabetic at the age of thirty-four, then I visited one dietician where I realized the power of food and its components. I reversed myself and till now I am very normal at the age of sixty-two."

After that episode, nutrition and its content lured me and I started working on it. For the next five years, I studied complete dietetics course and did many experiments. But I was fascinated by the fact that it is the elements at last that our cells utilize and channelize it to their varied use.

Using my previous knowledge of Physics and Chemistry I tried to make a formula that can channelize the nutrition to make many more uses from it. But I failed in doing so. Nonetheless, I found many other things that not only convert energy directly into other forms but also store energy in different forms. This is the reason, 'Why grasses of lawns are not mowed down by tyres as that stored kinetic energy of tyres as elastic energy, and when the tyre passed, it converted back its elastic potential energy into kinetic energy.'

Dragged by these talks, Hellry had forgotten about his fears and was convinced by his grandpa, so he surrendered and prepared himself for tests.

By performing several tests through varied machines some nicer looking ones and some very odd and dangerous-looking ones. However, Hellry underwent every examination and now his grandpa sat in front of three to four different monitors and examined the data.

A sharp smile grew on his grandpa's lips and in a short while, he excitedly said to Hellry, 'Congratulation Hellry!'. 'You can harness two types of energy right now, that is, Light and Heat.' Hellry was not able to understand as light and heat are very common to him. Hellry said with amusement and a bit of sadness, 'Means.'

'Oh! Oh! Sorry Hellry!', he said while removing and cleaning his spectacles. Turning towards Hellry he added, 'Let me explain. You can store and convert light energy. You can also store and convert heat energy.' His grandpa trying to clearly explain, looking distant as if he wants to look for an example, in a while said, 'Umm.... You just think that as you are a solar panel and .....' Hellry could not control himself and excitedly said, 'It means I can convert Sun energy into electricity and charge my car, power my house, etc.'

His grandpa laughing gently replied, 'No, Hellry it does not work like that but similar to that. And many more we have to find as these are very new.' 'Ok grandpa', quietly he said.

'As far as heat energy is concerned, you can take energy from any matter as everything stores energy in the form of internal energy which that matter losses or gains while changing its state, that is, solid to liquid or liquid to gas and vice-versa', explained his grandpa.

A feeble smile illuminated both.

# 4.

# Harvesting

Since a lot of time passed by then, his dad was very worried when he came to know that Hellry is with his father (Hellry's grandpa), as he never liked the principle of his grandpa which snatched his childhood. It was almost late evening, now Hellry's mother alongwith her grandmother completed cooking dinner and done almost all the household work. Now they too were worried, as everyone knows that Hellry's grandpa works in a mission mode, which means he will continue working until he finds a solution or has failed in all the attempts that he has planned beforehand.

The silence broke as Hellry's Grandpa entered the hall questioning his son, 'How are you, son?' All were stunned, even hellry's dad was shocked as his father never questioned him like this and never showed such a gesture to him. However, he replied hesitatingly, 'Fine. I am fine.' 'where is Hellry?' 'Where were you both? Even mom doesn't know about your whereabouts.' Hellry excitedly said, 'I am here, dad. And I am fine. I was with grandpa in his lab.'

'Dad, this is not good. Why have you taken him to your lab? You know that I hate your lab the most in this world as it has ruined my childhood

Grandpa slowly but seriously interrupted, 'Be calm. It is not like that. You know that my experiments were so different that the science community not paid much attention to them. So, I have to invest all my money and resources to start my lab and I have to find the result since no one was there to carry on my work. So, I insisted you sternly, to carry out my work.'

'But dad, you know I wanted to give my family all those things that I have missed in my life very much', Hellry's dad said emotionally.

It seems that today night, darkness is engulfing both sky and this room leaving everyone gloomy and in great despair. This gloominess was further enhanced when Hellry's grandpa suddenly retorted looking straight into the eyes of Hellry's dad, 'Do you think that all members of your family are happy?' He further added, 'We all do anything for the betterment of someone or atleast for self-pleasure. But in due course, we have to always think for the sustainability of our deed or decision.'

Hellry's grandpa walking towards the window, continued, 'My experiments are not for me. Even I was not sure whether I will see it happening or not.'

'Wait.. Wait. What you said, 'I was not sure.' 'It means you have made it successful.' Hellry's dad interrupted and stood from the sofa and walked towards his dad.'

Hellry's grandpa turning towards his son and looking towards Hellry said, 'Yes. Hellry made it.'

The room filled with astonishment and exclamation and many questions. Everyone has something to ask from both Hellry and his grandpa.

Before anyone would have said something Hellry's grandpa requested by his gesture to come with him. Everyone finding no other option, moved with him towards his lab where grandpa explained and showed them that Hellry has the ability to store energy and convert it into other forms. Heven excitedly said, 'Hellry do something. Some magic. Show us your ability.'

Her grandmom, while waving hairs of Heven, jokingly said, 'He is not a superhero. I think, he has to learn to use it.'

'Yes. From tomorrow morning I will help Hellry in using his abilities, added his grandpa.

That night was very long as everyone was in countless thoughts.

With the rise of the Sun, a new zeal and enthusiasm took over. Hellry and Heven was very excited as they were going to witness something unusual. They were chilled. However, Hellry's father was worried as well as still upset with all this.

Again with the whirling, beeping, and many other types of sounds, the lab was terrifying Hellry. Nonetheless, with everyone in the lab, Hellry is much more confident this time.

Hellry's grandpa asked Hellry to do certain activities, and in a few hours, Hellry acknowledged that he can use light energy and heat as per his wish and even transfer it to things attached to Hellry.

Then after Hellry kept on practicing and experimenting the whole day, while his brother saw everything with keenness and fondness and tried to understand the working principle of everything.

# 5.

# Laserboard

The next day, father, mother, and Heven left for the city leaving Hellry after a serious discussion between dad and grandpa.

Now Hellry was passing most of his time in the lab experimenting and noting, and the rest of the day in adoring the garden and watching television. His grandpa only use to guide him and inculcate a scientific discipline in him, as his grandpa reiterates, 'It is not important to find a result, but it is most important to document it and learn from those. As this will guide you that what else will certainly not work, saving not only your time and resources, but also of others who want to experiment in similar area.' Grandpa continued, 'Remember Hellry! Science is about sustainability of present and not about competition.'

Initially, it was tough for Hellry to understand but later because of continuous guidance he become habituated to it.

One day while watching cartoons, he jumped from his crouch and ran straight to the laboratory where he started documenting something. After an hour he ran back to his grandparent and handed over a piece of paper to him and asked, 'What do you think about this?'

'Umm...' Thinking hard, his grandpa asked, 'Please explain. I am not able to understand it.'

'Okay. Okay.' Hellry calming his excitement said, 'This is a laserbaord which will be powered by my ability to control light energy. This is the blueprint.'

Now grandpa looking seriously at that paper while raising his eyebrows and then putting over his eyeglasses. Now sitting straight while clearing his throat told hesitatingly, 'Nice. But...' He continued, 'No. It's okay. Have you thought about how to make it?'

Before the completion of the question. Hellry sharply replied, 'Yes. Sure.'

'Ok. Then let's go to the lab to work over it.'

With the help of a 3D printer they have printed the mechanical parts and attached them minutely and now they were prepared to check it.

Meanwhile, the speaker of the lab sounded, 'It's too late.' Now it is getting darker. Please have your lunch. This announcement was made by grandmom.

Without being late, grandpa looked towards me and we both went to the centre hall where grandmom was waiting for us eagerly. As she saw me she hugged me and kissed me with the same warmness and affection that she cherish to me every morning. I think this time it was the consolation for being late for lunch.

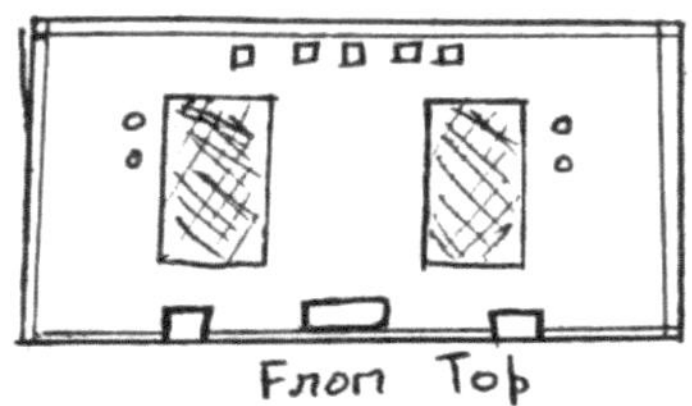


After lunch, as I stood to go to the laboratory, my grandmom insisted me to take a walk with her in the garden as soon darkness will spread over. Although I was enjoying her company and it was very pleasing to be beside her but thinking about my board kept me engaged. As soon as we returned back, I leapt for the lab.

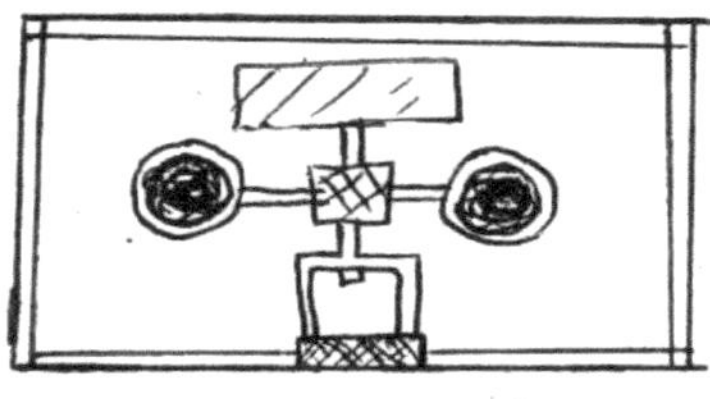


There I found that grandpa with my drawings alongwith many other drawings kept in front of him on his desk and with the help of a magnifying glass he was soldering some wires on the wings of the board. Seeing the seriousness of work, I controlled myself and moved very slowly like a cat preparing to pounce on mice and slowly touched the shoulder of grandpa. When he looked towards me, I asked him, 'How far we have reached?'

'Almost done, but still many things to check. That's why I have made all these designs for the possible changes that may be required,' replied grandpa.

While Hellry was checking with the design, his grandpa asked, 'Now you can check it.' Both walked in the garden, although it was dark, but in their excitement, they were curious to ascertain the result. So, Hellry kept the board on the ground and rode over it and started to power it by converting energy. 'It is working', shouted Hellry in excitement while lifting himself from the ground with laserboard. But soon dashed to the ground. He tried to do it again and again but he can't. By that time he was feeling very tired and desperate.

'Oh no. This is dark. It is using your energy. Leave it. We will try it tomorrow morning,' said his grandpa. Hellry was both excited and desolated.

The next morning, when grandpa went to the room of Hellry, he found that Hellry was not there. So, he rushed to the kitchen to look for Hellry as he is very fond of cooking that too with her grandmom. But there also Hellry was not present. Before he could have spoken something, her grandmom enquired, 'Where is Hellry? I haven't seen him.' Soon there was a loud noise. So both of them rushed in the direction of noise towards the garden. There what they saw kept both of them astonished. Their eyes widely opened. They paused.

Soon Hellry's grandmom rushed muttering while looking towards Hellry's grandpa, 'This is not good. How you can do this.' She inclined and helped Hellry who was still attached to his laserboard and lying semi-conscious on the grass. Her grandmom put off the helmet. 'I am fine. Nothing has happened to me as I have put on all the protective cover. I fell just because I was drained of my energy.'

Although his grandpa was concerned and felt responsible for everything, he was also thinking that how Hellry lose his energies so fast. He supported Hellry. Brought him inside, and served him his favourite soup alongwith some breadsticks.

My grandmom was continuously talking to me in order to make sure that I should not get bored and restless. While covering myself with a comforter and sitting on the sofa, I saw that my grandpa left us after some moment. I too want to accompany him but I can't, as still now I am feeling very tired. That complete day I took a rest while thinking that whether I can be able to hover with my laserboard or not. Is this the end of everything that we were trying to do? What if, if I failed? How my grandpa will feel. Many, many questions kept on coming to mind. But it was my grandmom whose continuous talk kept me engaged and now and then I was pretending as if I am listening to her. My grandpa also kept on coming and going in order to look me and, I think, to check me from getting frustrated.

In the evening, my grandpa with a warm smile asked me and my grandmom to come and follow him. Because of his so warm gesture, I gathered myself and walked with him towards his adorable garden, where while walking he told me which honked my brain, 'Success and failure are like two sides of the coin. If you flick a coin, you will get one. Please note that only one at a time. The more you flick there are more chances of getting any of the two. And it is also so sure that every time you will not get the same.' He continued, 'It all depends on you whether you keep on flicking the coin or you stop after some time.'

He furthered, 'There is a very minute difference between flicking a coin and working.' I curiously asked, 'What is that difference, grandpa?'

With a quick smile on his lips and both grandpa and grandmom looking gently toward me, grandmom replied, 'Planning.'

Now grandpa added, 'As in the case flicking coin you can't make any plan or strategy, but in case of any work you can do proper planning and form a strategy, decide your check-points by going through previous works, related works, associated works or even your intuition.' 'You can note it down in order to keep track and not get confused by afterward results. It will also check you from bloating with happiness on success or becoming desperate on failure.'

I took a deep breath and felt much relieved and energetic. The thought which kept me engaged throughout the day vaporized and now I promised myself to 'learn and do' only for doing and not for the result. As if my steps were correct then my result will certainly be achieved and if a fail to achieve then it means that I have to rectify somewhere. I will look back and correct it.

# 6.

# Mastering The Art

Two days have passed, and still, I have not touched that laserboard, no not because of fear of my last fall. But this time I am determined to follow the preaching of my grandpa. I want to learn from a different perspective. So, I studied a lot, gained much knowledge on the working of energies and its conversion and storage. I wrote every piece of knowledge that I gained. And after that on the third day, I made certain changes to my laserboard and with the help of my grandpa, I attached a piece of wire between my laserboard and my helmet which can make it responsive according to my wish.

Lastly, I was prepared to test it. I requested my grandpa hesitatingly, 'Can we test it.'

My grandpa allowed but he asked me to take the help of my grandmom too. I went to grandmom and requested her to come and help me. She nodded in 'yes!'

I put on all my protective wears alongwith that specially designed helmet and stood on that laserboard. And looking towards my grandmom and grandpa as seeking their permission. Understanding my desire, they both smiled and gave me a thumbs up to cheer me up and as a sign of best wishes. I lifted from the ground, this time I was taking the energy from Sun and channelizing it to laserbaord so I am feeling normal, not tired. I started hovering here and there in the garden. My grandpa gave me a sign to come down. I floated in the air and landed safely near my grandpa. He asked me to wait and he went inside. I guessed to his lab.

After some minutes, he come rushing with some devices and asked me to give him my helmet. He attached those. And handed my helmet back to me and through the movement of his eyes asked me to wear it again. While I was preparing myself to stand on the laserboard. I got terrified by a sudden voice coming from my helmet, 'Hello. Mic check. one, two, three. Sooner I realized that my grandpa fitted a communicating device in my helmet.' It has excited me a lot.

I, soon, took off and again started hovering around. My grandpa asked me to go high, but with caution. I started going up in the sky, this time I am not feeling any tiredness I become adept at harnessing solar energy like a plant and channelizing it directly to my board. My grandmom, too, was excited.

While hovering here and there, I felt that it still needs some advancement so that I can channelize this energy to any other object either directly or through my laserboard. I landed. I told my grandpa. While my grandpa was still thinking, my grandma, told since it is not possible to channelize your energy directly through your body, you can better try it to channelize it through your laserboard.

'Come with me. I will help you out,' said my grandmom. I was a bit perplexed as to how can she help me. Seeing this, my grandpa told, 'Don't worry. Your grandmom is a dietitian who treated me when I suffered from diabetes and later because of her utter desire to understand biomolecules and biophysics, we both shared and enhanced our knowledge.'

For the first time, grandmom accompanied Hellry to the lab. His grandpa was following him. When she reached the lab, she reacted, 'What have you made to this lab in these seven years? Nothing is arranged.' 'Where will I find my apparatus', she asked while looking towards grandpa. My grandpa a little reluctant and in despair, pointed towards a corner with his finger. My grandmom with a smile cheered up my grandpa and said, 'You thought that I will never come to this lab again.' On this, my grandpa replied, 'You left coming seven years back, and I left it two years after you.'

Both at the same time, 'No matter. We are here again.'

But Hellry wanted to ask although he could not that why they stopped experimenting.

Meanwhile, her grandmom carried a box toward the working desk. And with the help of grandpa opened it and took out some apparatus. She has her own design and paper, once again in purple sheet.

I excitedly asked, 'Is this the same one that I got...'

'No.'

'This is very different from that. That was step one and this is step two', retorted grandmom. She added, 'This is about how you can convert biomolecules into biophysics, it means how you channelize your energies.'

She passed almost two to three hours while studying those papers and later noting some key points and directed me to call grandpa from another desk where he was busy doing some other works and studying the design of my present laserboard.

'Listen, if we can add ports and a storage compartment on laserboard, then Hellry can store his extra energy which he can either channelize it to port or use it during the night so that his body should not get drained of energy', my grandmom explained it to my grandpa. He carefully looked for the figures, design and facts, then he shrugged his shoulder in confusion. Meanwhile, I understood as only the last night I was studying about the conversion of energy and change of phase of matter using energy. I supported my grandmom. And told her what little knowledge I have. On listening to this, my grandpa patted me and said, 'This is the real spirit of a scientist. As you don't have to only study or remember the facts, but you have to use it for its further development.'

My grandpa printed one unique storage box with his 3D printer and filled it with some gelatinous substance and connected it to the port. So now the whole connection is like this- my helmet - wire - laserbaord - storage box - port. It means that the energy that I will harness can be used either to carry my laserboard or if extra or laserboard not in use then that energy can be stored in the storage box, which can be directed through the port to outside.

‘Wait. There is a catch’, I shouted.

Both looked towards me in curiosity and bewildered towards me and asked, ‘What?’

I replied, ‘I can’t reverse energy stored in the storage box to laserboard to keep it powered in order to check my energy got drained when there is no external source that I can harness.’

'Oh yes', understanding the facts my grandpa replied and he gave a close look over the design and then bounced back towards my laserbaord and soldered another wire from my storage box to my helmet and connected it with the previous wire of my helmet with an auto switch and told me, 'This is an auto working switch which will start working when it will sense that there is no external source of energy.'

It's time to test.

We, again, gathered in the garden. This time much more confident and enthusiastic. Everything was working very nicely. I was able to channelize energy through that port and I tested it by directing visible light to those plants which were getting very few lights. All worked very well.

# 7.

# Secret Diary

I was enjoying very much with my newly designed and well-equipped laserboard. But I started noticing that now grandpa and grandmom stop talking and change the topic as soon as I reach near them. And they were much worried and confused.

At last, feeling it tough, I asked both, 'Is there any problem? I will not damage your garden or harm anyone or do anything which you feel will harm me. As you know that I never try to go out of the garden as you directed me.'

Grandma broke her silence and said, 'No. There is nothing like that. There is something grave that concerns us both, not because of you but because of the well-being and sustainability of the human race.'

'Leave it. Let's go for lunch, interrupted grandpa and questioned, 'What do you want to Hellry?'

Understanding the seriousness of the matter, I replied, 'No grandpa. Firstly you answer me then only I will take my lunch.'

'Don't be childish'

'No. I am a child. So, I can be childish.' 'Answer me.'

Looking towards grandmom as if he wants her to pacify me and change my mood. But my grandmom seems in a different mood.

On seeing this, my grandpa questioned, 'What will we answer to his dad? Try to understand this is not safe and till our child is very upset with us by letting Hellry know about all this, we will add distance between us. Even I don't consider it safe.'

'What is not safe?' I asked.

Besides answering me, my grandmom hold my grandpa's hand and in order to make him bold and decisive, asked, 'This is not about you or me or any family. This is for all families. We were trying hard to reach here only. And if we reached here, how can we turn back? Just because it is the Hellry who have done it.'

Grandpa hiding his eye contact and with distress told, 'There would be any other way out. We will work again on step one.'

'No way. It's not possible for us as the purple sheet had been lost. And in these years, we have withered ourselves', my grandmom answered with deep concern and a sense of inacapability.

I again interrupted, 'Please, for God's sake, tell me something and don't make me anxious.' I started feeling a sense of burning in my hand.

Before I should have noticed something, grandpa rushed towards the refrigerator and grandmom started hugging me and pacifying me. When grandpa returned with the ice pack and took my hand in his hand then I saw that there are crusting on the palms of my left hand. I understood that the energy which is a boon for me, is also a bane for me. As it can engulf me if I show some negative emotion like anger, frustration, anxiety, depression, etc. That must be the reason my grandmom passed her whole day with me when I fell from the laserboard, because she must be aware of it.

I took it as an advantage and becoming ignorant I tried to show myself as extra anxious and asked, 'Please answer me.'

Finding no other way, my grandpa surrendered. And from the shelf on which some antique articles were placed, he took a very old diary and dusted it. And while handing it over to me, smiled and said, 'Firstly calm yourself and eat something.' He enquired, 'will the thin-crust pizza with sizzling tomatoes and veggies be perfect for you?' While walking away, he said, 'I will add extra cheese for you.' On this grandmom shared a nice smile with me first and then looked gently toward grandpa.

Because of my enthusiasm, I wasted no time and started skipping through the pages of that diary. Since there were a lot of drawings, it attracted me a lot. So, I sat down straight and started to read it from start but the first few pages bounced over my head as it was talking about some dimensions and something of which I was not aware of. Later it has some weird-looking maps and some hand-drawn creatures with their details.

Meanwhile, grandpa came and sit beside me and handed over pizza to me and took his diary. While eating pizza, he told me that while in physics you have studied three dimensions, namely length, breadth and height. But accidentally while doing certain experiments with your grandmom, we discovered a fourth dimension. We named it klight. As it is the only reason, we sometimes feel that someone is passing beside you or seeing you, likewise.

'Hellry!' grandpa shouted, as I lost myself among the thoughts of ghosts and spirits.

With his sudden shout, one of the tomatoes of my pizza fell down from the pizza and was hanging with the help of cheese like a spider hanging from a web. I, now, thought that someone from klight has clicked my tomato to let it fall.

However, grandpa was still speaking seriously, 'Listen Hellry, it is important. There is a portal from where you can enter in klight. But the biggest issue is that there our energy exhausts very fast so we need an additional source of energy. That's why we were working on step one to harness additional energy so that we can survive there and do our experiments as well as know that place better.'

Grandpa continued, 'As you know that grandmom discontinued going to the lab. Let me tell you the reason, when we were experimenting. I went to klight where I found very weird characters that you have seen in my diary. Because of its weirdness and my enthusiasm, I tried to pass more time, but in due course, I got drained of my energy and I was about to collapse. Somehow your grandmom took me out from klight and she wanted to stay me safe. So, she insisted on me not to go there. And she stopped going to the lab as she was very sure that I can not do it alone.'

From then I have only these records that you are seeing in this diary.

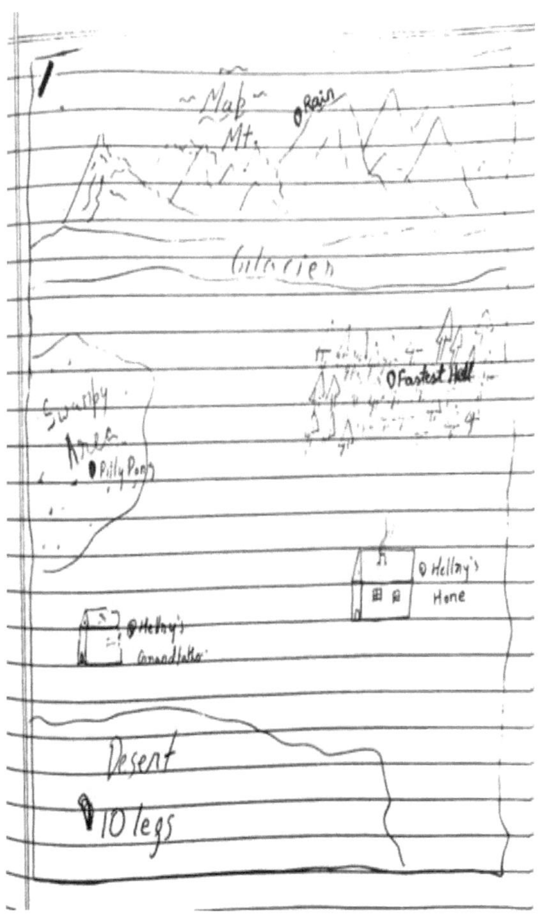

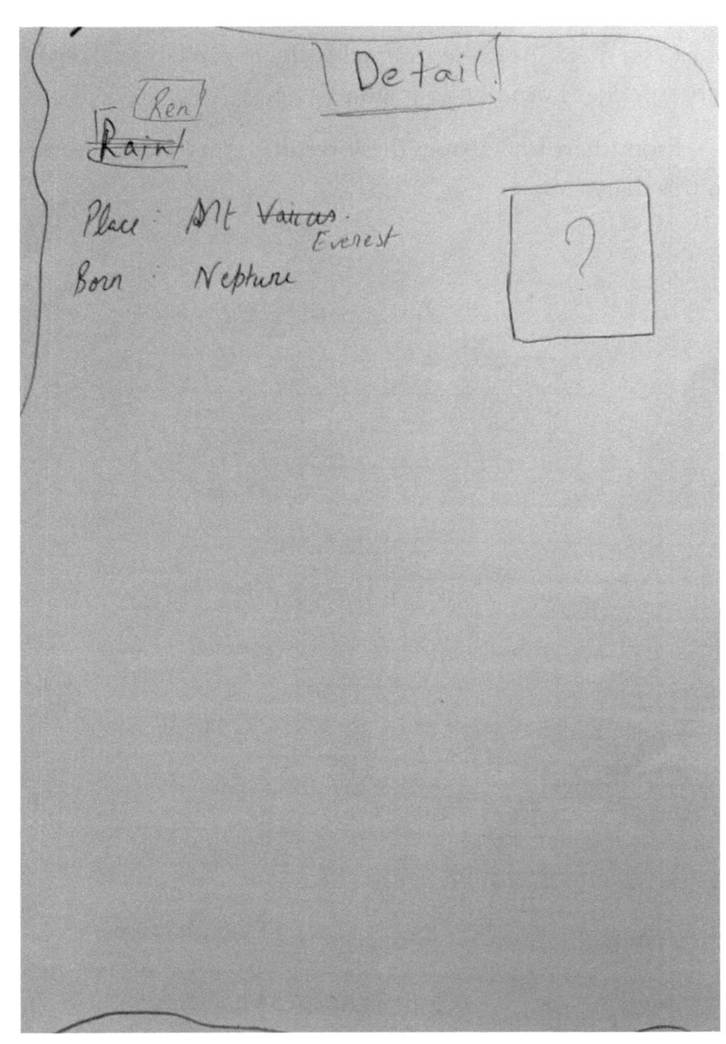
Detail
Ren
Rain
Place : Mt Everest
Born : Neptune
?

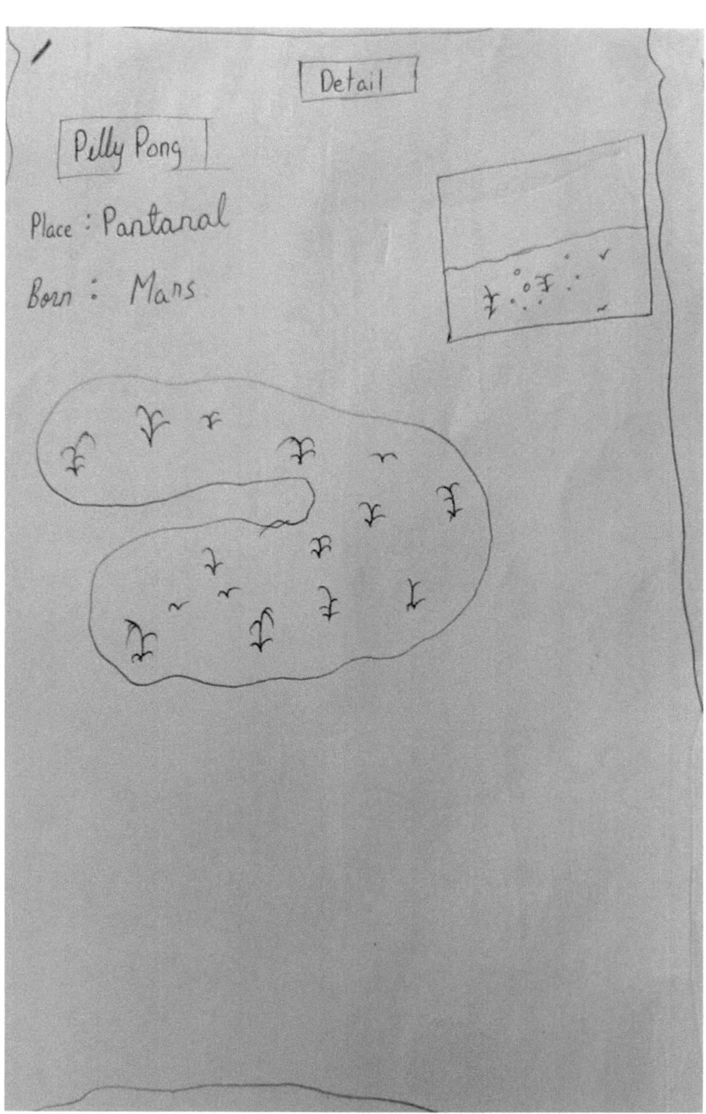
Detail
Pilly Pong
Place : Pantanal
Born : Mans

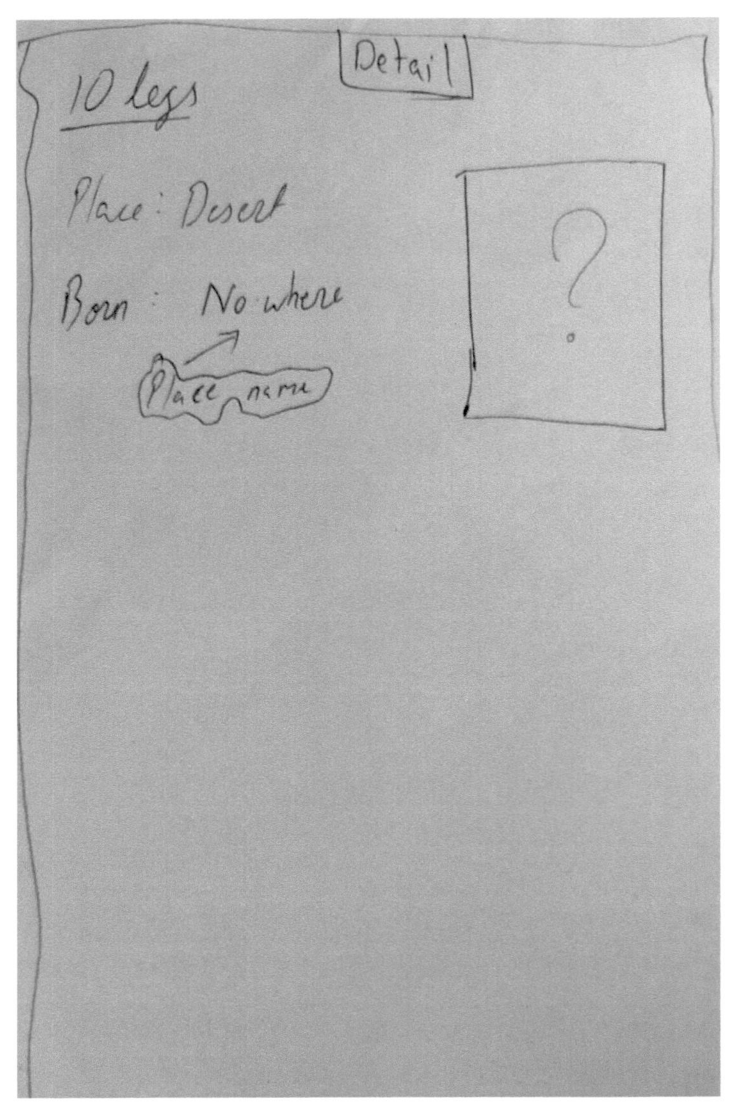
Detail
10 legs
Place: Desert
Born: No where
Place name
?

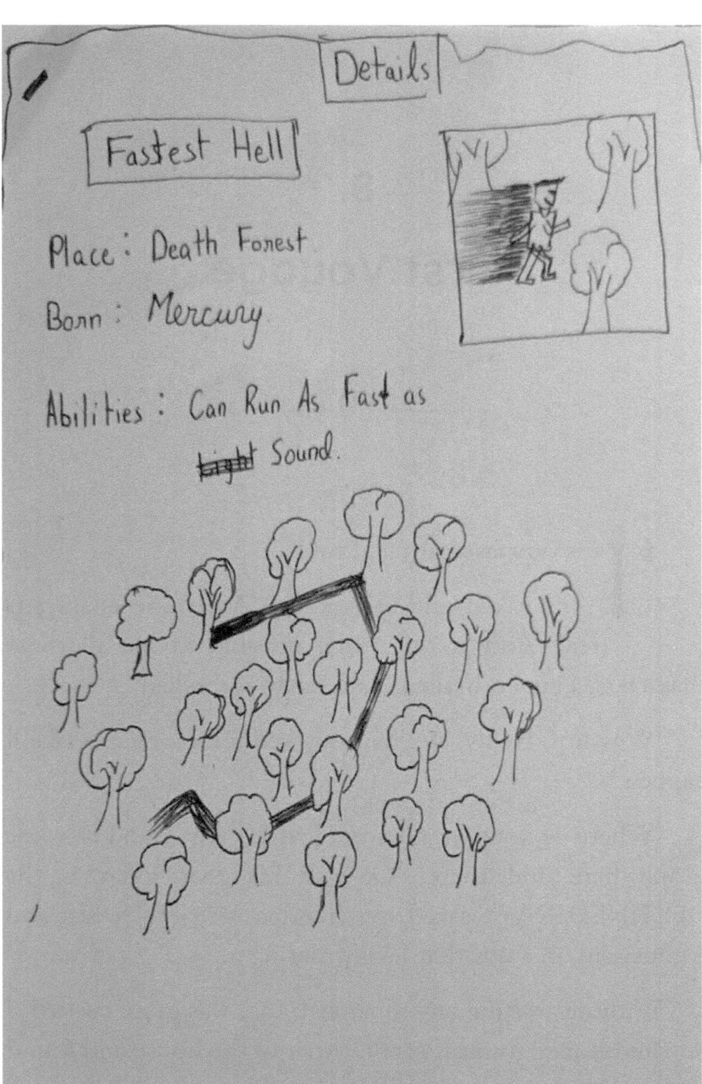
Details
Fastest Hell
Place: Death Forest
Born: Mercury
Abilities: Can Run As Fast as
~~Light~~ Sound.

# 8.

# First Voyage

'It is very fascinating', I told.

I asked enthusiastically, 'Are those characters real! And is this really possible to see all those characters? I am enthralled. I am really enthralled.'

'Why not, Hellry! We have worked for a long to make it happen.'

'Where is your grandmom?', asked my grandpa while gazing here and there. 'Go ask her that today is the DESTINED DAY', asked my grandpa with much zeal and enthusiasm, in a way that he is ordering me.

Without wasting any time, as I, too, was quite excited, I hop and leaped towards every corner of the house and found my grandmom and narrated to her, 'Today is the destined day.' Listening to this sentence, her eyes started blazing and she filled up with both energy and emotion and, like me, she moved as fast as she can towards the centre hall.

At the centre hall, now my grandpa was standing as if he was preparing himself and revising the last minute details. As I alongwith my grandmom reached the centre hall, my grandpa and grandmom looked towards each other with much more satisfaction than excitement. It seems that they have prepared themselves for this beforehand and have done their all homework. Although they seemed in perfect balance, but still yet I am a bit excited.

We hastily moved towards the lab.

There they showed me a large cylindrical box which is spherical at top and more or less looked like a large capsule. Before I could have asked anything, my grandmom told, 'Look Hellry, this is ‘k-way’, it is the portal from where you can go into the fourth dimension- klight. It is fitted with all the communication devices as one that grandpa has fitted in your helmet. Alongwith that it has equipment which will show your vitals that is your heart rate, pulse, oxygen saturation, body temperature as well as calorie count.'

While my grandmom was introducing 'k-way' to me, my grandpa was showing me each and everything it has and was pointing to me with the words of my grandmom. He further opened its door.

‘Wow!’ I exclaimed because it was really jawdropping.

I jumped inside and start touching but very gently each and every thing in that as I was trying to be familiar with all these.

My grandpa hold my hand and pulled me as if he wants me to come out of that. I followed him. I came out. Then he instructed me to go near the working desk. There, when, I reached, my grandmom handed over a digital watch-like instrument, and said that this is 'ketvig'. And told me, 'Hellry! ketvig is the remote controller of k-way and also a navigation system', she continued, 'You can not only locate your 'k-way' through this 'ketvig', but, also, drive it, even when you are away from it.'

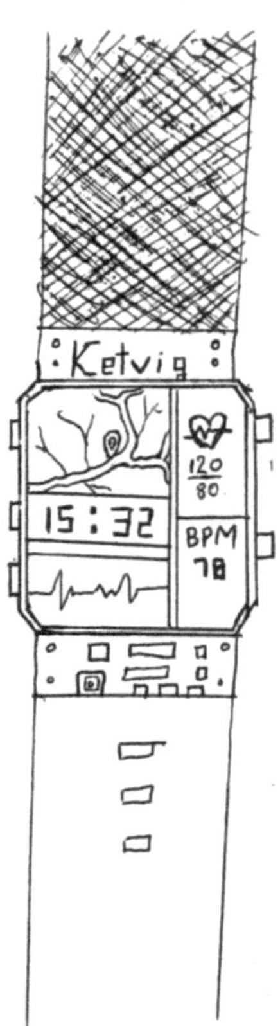


While explaining she hold my finger and pricked it with a lancet, I reflexly pulled my hand and cried in pain. But she again asked me, 'Don't worry. I need a few drops of your blood as I want to synchronize these devices with your biological identity so that only you can control it.' She gently took my hand in her hand, while my grandpa consoled me by putting his hand over my shoulder as to bolster me and make me brave enough, and gently squeezed my fingertip to let drops of blood ooze out which she put on the chip over the back of 'ketvig'.

All of a sudden, 'ketvig' start glowing and beeped two times. And in a computerized female voice said, 'Confirm identity.'

My grandma asked feebly, 'Hellry, tell your name.'

'Hellry'

'Okay, Hellry. Now I am your companion. I will receive energy either from your body or from your blood. So please try to put me on as long as you can to avoid pouring your blood in order to keep me awake.' Ketvig continued, 'Since I recognize your voice so I will always be listening to you and will send messages to the centre in case of distress or whenever you ask me to do so.'

As my grandmom handed over 'ketvig' to me. I put it over my wrist. It was looking nice. I make a certain change in it as per my preference, it was easy to do because I think it was either a modified digital watch or something based on that. So, it looked familiar to me.

'Am I, now, ready to go?', I asked excitedly.

Grandpa while looking towards grandmom in suspicion, shrugged his shoulder, cleared his throat and said, 'Umm... No. A big NO from my side.'

'Why grandpa!'

Grandmom shrieked, 'This is science.'

'You need to be neutral, which means no excitement or emotion. You have to rational', she added.

Grandpa coughed and clearing his throat said, 'You are not going on an adventure. You have to be meticulous. So instead of excitement inculcate a habit of being conscious.'

'Try to be empathetic, not judgemental.'

Although many things I don't got in my head, but I realized one thing that they are asking me to be calm and open.

I took a deep breath and said with depthness, 'Alright. I will be awake. I will be calm. And I try to be empathetic.'

'No. You can't say that I will TRY', grandpa exhorted while looking directly into my eyes. He added, 'Since we are on an extremely sensible mission, we have to adhere to the basic principle of mankind that is EMPATHY.'

Nonetheless, I want to clear up many doubts. But, merely I could say is YES. I will be empathetic while taking any decision.

'Okay! Let's prepare him for the ride', interrupted my grandmom.

So, now, grandpa checked every instrument while grandpa checked all my biological vitals and gave a positive nod as grandpa also signed for a Go-Go sign. Now they instructed me to sit inside it and waved to me. Just then grandma shouted, 'Stop Hellry.'

She ran towards a corner and collected my laserboard and come close to 'k-way' and put it in a corner and waved my hair gently with affection and with a warm cheer on her lips wished me, 'Have a safe and sound journey!'

Sooner, I clicked a few buttons as instructed by them.

With a feel of a sudden drowsiness and a light headedness, I felt that nothing has happened. I was just to switch another set of buttons, suddenly my 'ketvig' announced, 'Hellry, now you are in the klight dimension. Where do you want to go- To search for creatures of this dimensions or to explore while stepping out of your 'k-way'.'

I collected myself and decided to know its creatures first.

# 9.

# Friend Or Foe

Since speed always infatuated me so first of all I decided to see 'Fastest Hell'. So, I gave voice command to 'ketvig', 'Let's find 'Fastest Hell' first.'

With this command, I started feeling like I am flying with enormous speed. After some moments, when I become comfortable, I saw my 'ketvig' for navigation. I was surprised to see that it was moving at a speed of about fifteen hundred kilometers per hour. And I was traversing countries, mountains and rivers, even oceans and continents. Finally, my 'k-way' starts slowing and I was in California's Death Valley, the hottest place on earth and a graben. My dad told me that a graben is a down-dropped block of land between two mountains. It is just like a bowl.

Before 'k-way' should have landed, 'ketvig' announced, 'You are in the habitat of 'Fastest Hell'. Be alert, as it can move at the speed of sound.'

Soon 'k-way' landed and opened its door. I took my laserboard and came out to witness the klight dimension- the fourth dimension. I am the second person to do so, as the first is my grandpa. I was a little proud of myself because I am the first person to stay comfortable in this dimension.

However, I soon realized that I have to do many things. So I thought first to talk to 'Fastest Hell.'

'But, How?', this honked my mind. After a lot of brainstorming, I thought to locate it and follow it. I stood at my laserboard. And started searching here and there. But it was of no use.

I thought of a plan.

I made a cage of laser beams and covered it with ice. Then, since I was familiar that it can run very fast and I thought that when I will fire laser beams here and there, it will certainly try to find a safe place.

I started firing laser beams here and there, 'Fastest Hell' soon ran at lightning speed and searched for a safe place. And found the cage as its safer place, get inside it. And was trapped.

It was doing many unsuccessful attempts to break it. After say an hour or so, he felt tired and sat in the center of that cage.

Now I approached. Seeing me. It was astonished, as I was. It was almost looking like us, humans. Initially, I thought that how I will communicate with it. Many weird ideas are coming into my mind.

I thought to write and show it on placards. 'Wait. Wait. I don't have a paper,' I asked myself, 'Poor buddy. How can I miss that.'

Failing this I thought, 'Why not to use sign language or facial gestures.'

'Will I be able to make it?'

While all these thoughts were getting inside my head, I was about to reach the near cage.

'How you reached here? How can one break the barrier? Are you human or from any other place, a feeble voice comes?

It was 'Fastest Hell', who was saying my language.

Merely I was about to become comfortable and sigh in relief, a sudden burst of surprise took over. 'How can you speak our language? Would you be able to move in our dimension?', I asked in quick succession.

'No. But there are some times and some places, where I can feel, listen and rarely touch and move things in your dimension, humans refer to me, with love, ghost or spirit', it told me with pride.

It made me laugh.

'Why are you laughing', it asked with the same feebleness in his voice and a slow pace.

I replied, 'No. Nothing. We don't call you ghost or spirit with love.'

'Then'

'With fear. Utmost fear.'

'But I never harmed anyone.'

'I always try to keep people safe by moving things at places where we can do so or by crying loud thinking that even a faintest voice will reach.'

'Those places are called haunted in our dimension.'

'It is very weird', desperately said 'Fastest Hell'.

Soon my 'ketvig' buzzed and announced, 'Be fast. You might get late. A message from grandmom.'

Since we can not communicate in real-time, so we have to rely on either voice or text messages.

I again started thinking, about what to do with this creature- whether to set it free or kill it or keep it in the cage.

Since I have no other reason than fear of the unknown, in killing it or keeping it in the cage. So by being empathetic, as I am preached by my grandpa, I thought to put a radio-collar, by which I can not only locate it but also communicate with it or hear it.

Although it was hindering its privacy but a thought made me strong because our phones also do the same, everytime listening to us. That's why it wakes up and responds with the wake word.

So, I put that radio-collar asking it to be our first gift. On this, it promised me to come back as it also wants to gift me something.

We bid adieu to each other.

# 10.
# Pilly Pong

'Fastest Hell' followed me beside my laserboard and it seems that it is trying to walk as slowly as in order to give me company. We reached. I boarded and departed with lots of memories and thought.

And one thing was continuously making me laugh, that 'Fastest Hell' feels pleasure in being called a ghost or spirit.

As soon as 'k-way' departed, 'ketvig' asked, 'What or Where next?'

Since I was thinking of something else, I, spontaneously, said, 'Pinny Kong.' Correcting myself and with an order-like voice, I replied, 'Please navigate towards the habitat of Pilly Pong.'

'Okay, Hellry.'

Again a fast wheezing sound came and it seemed like I am soaring. Since I can't see outside so I looked at my 'ketvig' which again was traversing through mountains, rivers, country borders including the ocean. While I was lost in geography, revising what I have been taught in school and memorizing about the monuments in those areas through which I was passing. Meanwhile 'ketvig' announced, 'K-way is about to reach Pantanal, the biggest wetland in South America.'

Just then, I recalled about Ramsar convention, 'It is an international treaty on conservation and sustainable use of wetlands.'

Nonetheless, 'k-way' is about to reach. And I start preparing in my mind that what could happen and how I will react. I was thinking of my last strategy which worked well for 'Fastest Hell'. For a moment, I lost myself in nostalgia.

'Ketvig' announced, 'Welcome to Pantanal! Now you can find 'Pilly Pong. Since it can be invisible and make an army by regenerating itself. So, I will suggest you to land at the safest place, a little far from their habitat, that is, marshy places.'

'Okay then,' I answered, 'land at the best place that you find according to your data.'

In a few minutes, I felt that 'k-way' has landed. By informing me about the details and other things, 'ketvig' gave me a nod to open the door. So, I took my laserboard and thought that today it is going to be the most interesting day, as I can hover a lot on my laserboard. I checked for my bio-vitals in 'ketvig'. Everything is OK.

Now I asked 'ketvig', 'Let's find Pilly Pong.'

I started hovering around the Pantanal, it was amazing, having varied flora and fauna. Now I understood that why my geography teacher always tells us about the importance of wetlands.

Almost it is going to be dusk, now I started feeling restless. Only then, my only companion in that vast marshy area, ‘ketvig’ announced, ‘You have a voice message. Should I read it?’

'Yes, sure!'

'Come back! Start tomorrow fresh,' a message from grandpa.

Since I too was tired, so I asked ketvig, 'Bring 'k-way' to this place.'

With a sound of ‘Okay Hellry' and a few minutes, 'k-way' was there. So, I boarded and put my laserbaord in the specified corner and closed my eyes. And asked to myself, ‘Let’s return to normal dimensions.’

‘Ketvig’ replied, ‘No. I cannot do it. You have to do it manually or it can be done from the lab.'

Though I was reluctant to switch on the buttons, I switched on the guided buttons and sat on my seat.

Again, I felt drowsy and shivered a bit.

And this time, ‘k-way’ announced, ‘Welcome back, Hellry. You can open the doors.’

Before I would have opened the door, the door got widely opened. My grandparents in quick succession hugged me, kissed me and they were very excited to see me. With this warm and homely welcome, my tiredness went away and I started feeling very special and cherished. My grandmom was holding my favorite drink. She handed it to me and my grandpa hold my hand and took me out of 'k-way' and guided me to the central hall, where he had placed a pizza of my choice with a thin crust and a lot of veggies hidden in cheese.

We all sat together. They were cuddling me and showing their affection. It was very pleasing for me and it seems as if this cannot be found anywhere and cannot be bought from anywhere. So, this is very special. It is amazingly special.

# 11.

# Finding A Way Out

The next morning brought not only zeal and enthusiasm but also a question in me that how can I find the Pilly Pong, as it might become invisible upon seeing me and it can be dangerous to me if it creates an army of its own kind. With all these questions perturbing me and keeping me busy, I heard a loud noise coming from the lab. I rushed towards the lab, where I found that my grandpa has hurt himself while tinkering with an old and rickety box, and in pain, he shouted.

Meanwhile, grandmom also arrived, we both helped him in putting ointment and bandage over his wound and it seems that he would not be able to work well with his right hand.

'How you injured yourself,' grandmom asked, 'are you now okay.'

Looking towards me, grandpa said, 'Leave me. Prepare Hellry for today's expedition. Today is a very important day.'

'But before that please try to open this box,' grandpa added.

We both, grandmom and I, asked together in bemusement, 'What is in this box?'

Grandpa said, 'Open it first. Then only you can understand, what I will say to you.'

His reply left us more bewildered. Grandmom took that box and looked at it from all sides and tried to open it. It seems that it is snugly fit. I, too, was giving a keen look in that box and at the activities of my grandmom.

Later, I realized that the cover is made of metal while the box is made up of plastic. So, a quick idea honked my mind, that metal can expand on heating. I asked to my grandpa, 'Will heating affect the inner content.'

'NO. Not at all,' grandpa said and was questioning me, 'Why are you asking this?'

But, sooner, I left them and went to the desk and switched on the water bath and gently asked my grandmom to pass on that box.

She came near me and understood that, what I am going to do.

She handed it to me and in a feeble and concerned voice said, 'Be careful. It's hot.' And passed on oven gloves to me.

Meanwhile, grandpa was also there, and seeing that my idea is going to work, he forget about his pain and took the box from the water bath and opened it lightly and carefully.

We all look into that box as if some magic is going to happen. We all were very excited. But what's that? It has a jelly-like thing.

In a distress, I asked, 'Ohh... This is jelly. You might have kept it for me. Now I am a grown-up, grandpa. I don't like this that much that you can hurt yourself that too on a day when I have to go for the most arduous task, catching an invisible creature.'

'No. No. Hellry,' grandpa interrupted me and looking directly into my eyes said, 'this is not jelly that you eat. It is a pheromone jelly that will not only attract Pilly Pong but also make it visible.'

He further added, 'But be very careful in using it. As this is very sticky for a human.'

Grandmom heard it and gave a gentle smile and asked, 'But how will you help Hellry today as you have hurt yourself.'

Grandpa smilingly said, 'Today I will guide you and Hellry will do the work. Now we are getting late. Get him to the 'k-way'.'

With a kiss, he bid adieu to me. Now again I opened the door and sit inside and closed it and like the previous day my grandmom showed a loving gesture and departed. And I switched on the buttons and with the same drowsy feel, I arrived in 'klight'.

'Ketvig' asked, 'Hellry, should I go to the same place where we were last time?'

I answered affirmatively.

Now I took my laserboard, and started hovering Pantanal. But this time despite of looking over the varied flora and fauna, I am focussed on finding a place that would be hard to reach for me yet easy to catch 'Pilly Pong'.

'Wait. Wait. There is a small trench,' I said to myself. And directed my laserboard over it and put that jelly with the help of a spatula.

To my surprise, in a fraction of a time, there started appearing bubbles. And in the blink of a moment, a large area got filled with bubbles- some large and some small. Some look cute while some are terrifying. All have different colours. Even some changing their colours.

Till now I am trying to collect myself, I felt that something very big is rising behind me and is going to cover me. My 'ketvig' screamed, 'DANGER! DANGER! Move to a safe place.'

But where to find a safe place.

Everywhere is the same thing. Although I moved a little farther and looked back. My jaw dropped open. It was both terrifying and soothing, really difficult to explain. It was looking like small to large oval to capsular shaped brightly colourful bubbles are arranged over each other and were growing. I got a bit confused, too. It was not looking like a creature. It was more looking like a lather of soap. For a few seconds, I reached to my bathroom, where I use to play with these lathers and blow them. Suddenly, I got an idea to blow it or freeze it. I preferred to freeze it as I can take energy from any substance so I started drawing energy from that bubble-like creature, probably Pilly Pong.

It stopped growing. But it kept on growing from another side. I turned towards that side, and I froze it, too. In quick succession, I moved around and kept drawing energy. In physics classes, it was very tough for me to understand the concept of conversion of state of matter or phase of matter. But now, I can understand it clearly that if energy is taken away then the body will cool down and freeze.

Soon I thought that what I am doing because now I am surrounded by big mountains of static lathers and it is tough to predict what can happen next. I asked, 'Ketvig. Is this Pilly Pong? Confirm.'

With beeping and buzzing, 'ketvig' answered, 'Biological confirmation is affirmative.'

But how can I talk to it? It does not look like a creature. No mouth. No arms. Nothing. Is this like bacteria? Unicellular? Oh God, where do I get stuck? What to do next? Do I have to kill them? Will it speak? But how can it speak?

Just then I heard, 'STOP. Don't freeze us. I will die.'

It surprised me, I looked in the direction from where this sound came. I found that there was nothing, only some small bubbles continuously changing their shapes.

'I can talk to you as I can create transverse waves by changing my shape, which you can perceive,' another sound came, 'please don't harm me, as I am not your enemy. I just want to protect myself by terrifying you.'

'Okay!' I shouted looking here and there and pretending as if I am neither confused nor terrified. But, actually, I am very bewildered and also thinking that how will it listen to me.

'Thanks for your generosity!'

'I am not new to you or humans. Even a normal humans can see me when they close their eyes on a bright sunny day and I appear to them as a string of small bubbles in the red background. I enjoy playing, so when they move their eyes, I can go up and down or left and right.'

I recalled that I also use to do this when I feel upset or in case of boredom. I asked then why you were trying to terrify me.

'Because you humans are very unpredictable. You seem to be alienate every good thing from yourself in order to have bad, unsustainable things that will harm your posterity and will put your existence in doubt. So, I was just trying to keep this dimension free from your encroachment.'

'If you are satisfied with me and feel that I will not harm you then please thaw me.'

'Ketvig' interrupted, 'Its physical response suggests that it is not lying. Hellry, you can trust it.'

I started thawing it. It also absorbed its own type and now only one bubble remained. Pilly Pong promised me that when I will need help in klight, it will help me. With these words, I collected that pheromone jelly with the help of a spatula because it will not allow Pilly Pong to move anywhere as it will always be attracted to it. It also told me that I don't go invisible, my molecules just merge with the environment.

As you are made up of cells. And cells are made of molecules and molecules are made up of elements. So, when you can disintegrate yourself, you can spread yourself and become invisible. This jelly attracts our molecules, making us cohesive, thus we can't spread.

There were no shaking hands as Pilly Pong has no arms.

# 12.

# Snow Balls

The day was still left. With a lot of positivity, I thought to go explore further. Of the four creatures, I have met with Fastest Hell and Pilly Pong. And the other two beings, Ten Leg and Ren, having contrary habitats- desert and mountain, respectively. Since the tropical climate of Pantanal exhausted me, so I preferred to have a snowy trek. Therefore, I asked 'ketvig', 'Please go to Mount Everest. As I want to know more about Ren.'

Ketvig replied, 'Would you like to board 'k-way from here or go to that place where we have landed.'

Pantanal was so adorable that I want to have one more look at its plants and animals, thus I preferred to hover and went to k-way and boarded it.

Again, I started looking at my ketvig's navigation because I know that it was going to be the most interesting journey as I am going to traverse one whole continent that too Plateau Continent, Africa. And the world's largest peninsula, Arabian

Peninsula. Two oceans- South Atlantic Ocean and the Indian Ocean. It is really going to be thrilling. Although I can't see because my k-way has no glass pane nonetheless I can feel it through my ketvig. Thanks to it.

While traversing the Atlantic Ocean, I was thinking that will it become the world's largest ocean one day as it is increasing in size while the Pacific Ocean is shrinking. And, if yes, how long will it take? Certainly not in decades, but in centuries or millions of years.

As then I crossed it and was passing over Africa, the cradle of humankind. African Bush elephant, the largest and heaviest living land animal. The longest river, the Nile.

The Rub' al Khali, also called 'the Empty Quarter', in the Arabian Peninsula is the largest sand desert in the world and has sand dunes as high as about Eiffel Tower.

I was lost thinking about the stormy and dusty winds called haboob, just then, ketvig announced, we are about to reach. I looked at my ketvig. I was traversing the Himalayas. A place where once the sea, Tethys sea, use to happen is now the world's highest mountain.

'You can now step out, but be cautious as outside it is very cold and stormy. Maintaining your homeostasis may drain additional energy so keep drawing energy. Draw energy from the light source, as if you draw energy from heat then it will further decrease the temperature of your environment,' warned ketvig.

As usual, I took my laserboard and eyewear and windcheaters and stepped out. After walking for some distance, my ketvig alarmed me, 'Caution! You are going to approach a big metallic object.' I thought, 'How could it be possible that at this peak, anyone will carry such a heavy metallic object? Even it can't be an aeroplane because of two reasons- first, they avoid flying over it. Second, it is cylindrical in shape. But here it is almost triangular. I asked, 'So, what to do?'

'Hellry! with caution and alarm, you can proceed. But stick to your laserboard,' replied ketvig. A thousand questions are arising in my mind. Fear of uncertainty is hounding me. Looking here and there, going slow, finally I approached near that thing. I tried to strike it in wanting to confirm whether it is metal or not. As metals are sonorous. But there was a thick blanket of ice over it. Failing in that, I have only option to find a place where I or ketvig can acknowledge that what is this.

I reached its corner or vertex. I carefully moved and turned. To my surprise, a light is coming out from the centre. It appears as it is a door that opens upward giving a portico-like look. I guessed that it must be a vessel, probably from another planet.

'Oh.. It means that it is Ren's ship from which it would have traveled from Neptune,' I thought.

Only then, ketvig interrupted, 'This is Ren's ship.'

'Yes. I guessed that.'

Next what. I approached cautiously towards that door. I saw that a huge giant figure was sitting only at the gate. I started drawing light energy and storing it in my cube. So that in case of emergency, I can use it either to escape or to counterattack.

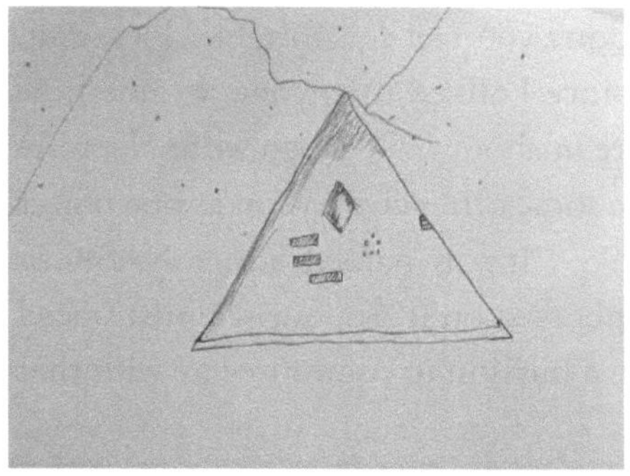

I was totally stunned when I heard, 'Welcome Hellry!'

'How can it know my name? Can it travel in my dimension? Does it know everything about me? Whether he is a friend or a foe? Is it challenging me?'

'Don't be surprised. I heard your name when your device warned you quoting your name.'

'Don't think much. Come inside. It would be very cold for you outside.' And a giant hand came out from the door directing me to come inside.

I hovered near the gate and was just going to enter the gate, meanwhile, ketvig warned me of the uncertainty. Ignoring it, I entered the door. There was a tall figure with a body having three segments namely the head, thorax, and abdomen, mostly like us. But have many appendages- one pair of small limbs from its head, which is very unusual in animals, as animal's cranial appendages are sessile like the horns of deer, and others pair arising from the abdomen like ours. It has a pair of antennas like a cockroach having an ear-like ending on both. It is comfortable in walking on either four legs or only hind legs.

Ren told me, 'Why don't you feel comfortable? Please sit. A long time has passed since I talked to anyone. I came here some three decades before in about 1990 when we at Neptune sensed that there must be some other civilization as one object crossed our planet in 1989. It was named either NASA or Voyager, as both were embossed on it. So, our scientist traced its origin and send me on a mission to communicate with that civilization.'

'Coming here I found no trace of any civilization. When I communicated with my science community, they told me to take shelter at the best-suited place. So, I found this place as homely as it is cold as you might be knowing that Neptune is very cold,' continued Ren.

I interrupted, 'Why have you not chosen Antarctica, the coldest place on this planet.'

It continued, 'From which planet do you come? Are you a scientist? You have a small stature. Are you younger or this is the normal height of your species?'

I preferred to hide my identity so I replied that I am from planet Mercury and this is our average height. And I can harness light and heat energy.

Ren said, 'It's very nice. It means you don't need to eat like us. For harnessing energy, we have to depend on certain things as we can't obtain them directly. I think it is tough for you to understand.'

'I have been here for such a long year on this planet and found no signs of life, although it has rich and varied elements which can form a variety of molecules. Now I found you that too from Mercury. Tell me something about your species and planet and the purpose behind coming here,' it went on speaking and asking.

Quickly I answered, 'Same here. Our planet's orbit observed two unidentified objects which were not looking similar to any natural object. Thus, our scientists traced it and found that it is something like spacecraft but there was no sign of life, which enthusiast us to know more about it. We followed it and found the same name NASA but in spite of Voyager, on one Parker Solar probe and on other, Solar orbiter was written. Finding it artificial, our quest for gaining more insight into that arose. Thus, I am here.'

'Coming here, I found you and no other being. I think the main species of this planet would be living inside the surface like burrowers,' I further added, 'Okay! It's nice to meet you. Now let me return, as the climate of this planet is hostile for me.' With these words and in quick succession, I hovered my laserboard and departed as quickly as possible. And now I am very excited to meet Ten Leg, as these creatures are very interesting and have a lot to share.

I boarded my k-way. Asked ketvig to move towards the habitat of Ten Leg. It lives in Deliblato Sands, the largest sand desert in Europe. Within a few minutes, ketvig announced, 'We are about to reach.'

And on our arrival, ketvig, as usual, cautioned me, 'Sand dunes can be dangerous. It can rise up to 200 metres. Apart from that, Ten Leg can extend its leg.'

With these terrifying words, I opened the door and took my laserboard and asked ketvig, 'To trace the biological mark of Ten Leg.' Ketvig scanned the area fastly as it is a vast open area and showed the direction. I hovered in the given direction and in minutes, some faint images of Ten Leg, I saw. I took out my magnifying device, more like a binocular, and I was astonished it was holding an animal and was about to tear it apart in order to eat it. It was its prey. I, initially, thought of saving that prey. Sooner, I recalled the words of my grandpa that BE EMPATHETIC. I stepped into the shoes of Ten Leg and thought I, too, am a non-vegetarian, so what can Ten Leg can do if it is a carnivore? It is its food habit, much like a lion and tiger. I paused for a moment in order to complete its food. When I was sure that it has completed its meal then I proceeded but with caution as now I am well aware that it is a carnivore and may harm me considering me as its food.

I planned to capture it first, but it may bring animosity between us. This thought perturbed me. So, I started thinking of other plans.

After a lot of brainstorming, I come up with a plan that if I cool the surrounding then it might get stupefied and, in that state, it may not be able to plan on capturing me and making me its prey.

Thereby I started drawing energy from the surrounding in order to cool it. In the extreme case, I can, also, use this energy as a defensive measure. As per the plan, I cooled the environment. And, wow! I was right I saw from the distance that Ten Leg started looking here and there in astonishment that what is happening. Seeing the right moment, I moved close to Ten Leg. For seeking its attention, I shouted, 'Ten Leg!'

It looked towards me in great surprise and started thinking something.

I, without any delay, asked, 'Don't be astonished. I am your friend from another planet.'

Meanwhile, I recalled that it came from Nowhere, a planet in another galaxy, and it can regenerate its legs, even make it long and has the only weakness, that is, its eyes.

'FRIEND! What does it mean?' growled Ten Leg.

I stammered, 'Friend... Friend means a person who can help you.'

'Oh. It means you can send me back to my planet. Of course.' It added, 'Then send me, here things are very ugly. I don't have any, what you call, friend. Any friend, here? After a long time, I have spoken to anyone.'

I was about to correct myself about the definition of 'friend' but Ten Leg's emotions stopped me from doing that. Now I was lost in analyzing how can I really help Ten Leg in sending it back and suddenly many questions honked my mind like how it reached here. Why did it come? And likewise.

I interrupted, 'How did you come here and what was your purpose of arrival.'

'NO. No. I never tried to come here. I alongwith my pals, same as your friends, were having a spacewalk, and I was a bit naughty and unruly, so I told them that I can walk in space without having the tying knots. I untied myself, although my pals were asking me not to do that. But I untied myself and drove my space scooter at full speed. The steering cables of my space scooter broke, so I was not able to steer it back. I don't know for how long and how far I traveled. But in the last, when I was about to lose my all hopes of survival. My space scooter started wheezing and speed up with great speed and I felt enormous heat which even brought some scars on my outer layer as this was something very unusual to us as we can sustain heat upto 2000 degrees Celsius. Within about 30 seconds, I felt that I was about to touch some surface, so as we were taught to deaccelerate on approaching surface, I opened the parachutes of my space scooter, but it was of no use. So, I understood that the atmosphere of this planet is enormous that's why it is attracting us with that speed, it means either this planet is very small or is very dense. Finding no other option, I extended my five legs upward and opened it like a wing and with the rest of my five legs, I flexed it and recoiled it like spring so that it can bounce me up when I touch the surface.'

With a deep heart, he overwhelmingly said, 'So I reached this planet. Finding this planet very cool, I started looking for the hottest and most favourable place, I come here, as this place is hotter and lot of sand where I can take shelter, unlike the Death Valley which is, of course, the hottest place but is barren.'

'From then to now, I am totally stuck here. I don't know how to get back. Even I don't know which way is my planet.' It continued, 'Here, I found some creatures from whom I can essential nutrients.'

'Will you help me?'

I tried to startle it but now I was totally in a fix that what should I say to it. I was totally aware that it is very tough for the best of the scientific community of earth to send him to its planet. Leave sending, even to find its planet in this vast universe. Again, my definition of 'friend'. What a silly mistake, I have committed.

Again, it interrupted, 'Tell me. You will help me, will not?'

'Certainly....' I answered abruptly.

Finding no other way, I thought it would be best to stick to my word, so I cleared my throat and with energy, I said, 'Certainly, I will help you. But before that, I have to find your planet and for that, I have to know that from which direction you came and for how long you traveled and with what speed you traveled. So that I can calculate the distance and find your planet and help you travel safely without a mistake. But all this will take time. So please allow me to leave for now. And I will come back with my scientific instruments.'

With my logical words, it pacified itself and bid adieu to me.

# 13.

# Back To Home

Questions and questions everywhere. I think, it was the biggest day of my life. Full of adventure. Full of revision of texts that I have been taught in class, told by parents, and seen on the web. Full of surprises. The world, we think is not enough, there are many things beyond it, but it seems very true that physics and chemistry are the same. Thanks to my interest in these core subjects which helped me a lot in understanding these.

I reached near my k-way hovering on my laserboard and asked ketvig to open the door and boarded it. Pressed the buttons with a very pleasing feeling as I have not harmed any creature. I am very excited to see my grandparents as I have to tell them a lot. With the same drowsy feel, within a few seconds, ketvig asked me to open the door as we are at home.

I opened the door.

What's that? I was awestruck.

No one was there to receive me.

'Has grandpa felt seriously ill because of the accident that happened in the morning', I asked to myself.

No, it can't be that serious as that was a minor cut.

But... what then happened!

Am I travelled across time? Is this any other dimension-fifth or something like that? I tried to assure myself, so I asked ketvig, 'What's the date and time?'

'It's 7 PM and today is 8th January, 2023.'

I calmed myself. But then, why no one is here?

I was moving very slowly, gazing at each and every machine and desk suspiciously. As a bad thought came into my mind that some portal might have opened, from where creatures from the fourth dimension, klight, can travel here. And have done some harm.

Suddenly, I heard, 'Wow! Hellry it's you.' And someone from the back hugged me. The hand was small like mine.

Oh, I guessed, it's Heven.

'I am waiting for you since noon as I have to tell you a lot of things and show you something that you will really admire,' Heven said in continuity and excitedly.

I forget about all the day's adventure and, really telling, I am not very happy seeing Heven here. I don't know, why, but I am not happy either because of jealousy or anything else or fear.

Before I could have uttered anything, he took out his camera and hold my hand and dragged me towards a chair and gestured for me to sit. He sat near me and switched on his camera and opened the file.

He was in such haste that he gave me very little or no time to think or ask anything. He showed me photos of some odd-looking machines and a space-type suit. And then he told me that he made all this in his newly set up lab that too in our room at home.

I was about to ask something from him. But he interrupted, 'What were you doing in that room.' He continued, 'Is it some sort of special lab or diagnostic area or practice section?'

His question made me understand that he does not know about anything about klight, ketvig, or k-way.

So, now this time, I interrupted Heven and asked him sternly, 'Where are grandpa and grandmom?'

'Oh. They are in the centre room with mom and dad. They told me to wait there and directed me that if anything buzzes or any signal comes then call them without delay. And they also instructed me to not touch anything.' He continued, 'When I come here, I found this fairytale-like diary so I was passing time reading it. It is very interesting, you should also read it. It talks about weird creatures like Ten Leg, Fastest Hell, .....'

I left Heven in between and moved towards the centre hall. Heven shouted from behind, 'Wait. As they ask to wait here only.'

Without looking behind and while moving, I answered, ‘They asked you to wait.’

‘No. For both of us.....’

I was about to reach the centre hall, when some voice started coming from the centre hall. So I slowed down in order to ascertain that what they are talking about.

'.....not about the future of one child. It's about science. About world. About many things that I can't tell you or explain to you. I am just trying to put myself since noon, but you are struck at the same point.' It was my grandpa's voice.

I understood that they must be discussing about me. I thought it would be like adding fuel if I go there. Or they may end their discussion seeing me. I felt that my interruption will end the discussion.

So, I moved faster and entered the room in a hurry pretending as if I am coming straight and I was totally unaware of their discussion.

I wished everyone. And moved straight to mom and hugged her then near dad and after that settled in between grandpa and grandmom. My grandmom hugged me and kissed me and asked gently and feebly, 'Is everything alright? Have you enjoyed it? We are sorry that we were not there to receive you or asked about your well-being for the whole long day.'

She, while seeking a response through my eyes and posture, stood up and asked, 'Get ready for dinner. I am going to serve it.'

Everyone moved from their place and started preparing themselves for having sumptuous and healthy food as my grandmom is not only a dietician but also enjoys cooking, as she always says that cooking is not only an art but a science too.

I am very happy from within. It was the greatest adventure of my day as I ended the discussion. I was feeling very proud. Just then I saw Heven.

I went near Heven and asked, 'Tell me, what you were telling me.' And again he started explaining to me many things- some ridiculous. 'Wait. Nothing is ridiculous,' I asked to myself.

As our dinner was about to end, my dad asked me and Heven to go to bed.

I asked, 'Dad! But..'

'GO TO BED, after dinner,' my dad ordered.

Grandpa intervened, 'Don't be so rude. Don't drag them.'

And slowly directed me and Heven to go.

We both went inside. Heven was so lost in his world that he was not ready to pay any heed to the things that are going around.

Although feeble voice was coming and sometimes it was so clear that I can understand and make the whole sentence and paragraph before and after that. So, it was annoying me a lot. Within a few minutes, Heven slept. My sleep was far away. The discussion was piercing me because I can't blame either my dad or my grandpa, neither I am angry nor distressed. I am just annoyed, not because they were having a discussion but because I can not put my words to them.

'BE EMPATHETIC' is really a magic pill that can calm any negative emotion and help think rationally.

I can understand that my dad is worried simply because of his childhood and his care toward me. And my grandpa is thinking about mankind, which obviously includes me and everyone, even my child and their child.

The only difference is that they are either not able to present their viewpoints or they are so stubborn that they don't want to hear other points. My conundrum is that I can't intervene. The first reason is I am the sole subject of the topic. The second one, I am a child of merely twelve years, it does not matter that my understanding and way of presentation can amicably resolve it.

As it is getting darker, so I am. With every minute, my annoyance was increasing and I started feeling as if I am chained. When things are becoming ugly to hold on then I decided.

I decided to find solace.

But where?

Might be in klight. A place where there is only nature and no trace of the living organism. Of course, bigger one. Visible one.

This idea brought a sense of energy in me and I hop from my bed and went directly to the lab and done all the necessary procedures in order to start k-way and leaped into the k-way, and closed the door. Took a deep breath in relief. And for a few seconds sat calmly holding the sitting handles firmly. Then breathed heavily. Finally asked ketvig, 'Take me to a place in klight, where there is no trace of the living organism.'

'Sorry! There is no such place where there is no living organism as bacteria can thrive in the hottest spring, sulphur beds and even in salt pans,' answered ketvig in its same machine-type accent.

I corrected myself, 'Okay. Okay. Then. Take me to a place where there no visible living organism thrives.'

With the same drowsy feeling, and sudden shaking and wheezing, Ketvig announced that now you can open the door, you are in klight.

I slowly opened the door and gently look forward. Although it is night but because of the vast open field with ripened grasses, it is looking like that a silver foil has been placed because it was a full moon night. Almost everything is visible. It was mesmerizing. I was totally stunned by this lustrous beauty and the unimaginable gift of nature.

For the first time, I used ladders of k-way, leaving behind my laserboard, and stepped down and touched the silvery grass. I walked forward, thanking my ketvig. After walking for some time, I saw a lake, which was appearing as if it is filled with milk. And a cool, soothing air is blowing around it. I sat down there on the grass and for some time I was just admiring the scenery.

Sitting there I was recalling my day. Many questions were there in my mind like- How do they understand my language?

After a few moments, grandpa and dad's discussion strikes my mind and has waned everything. Now, nothing was there that can please me. In a state of confusion and annoyance, I started pelting gravel in the lake. The sound that it creates and the silvery ripples, both were keeping me engaged and keeping me distracted from my negative thoughts.

By now and then, I was asking some fun facts or laws or theories of science and geography from my ketvig.

As I hold one disk-like gravel, about double the size of a biscuit, and was about to throw it, feeling that it might make a very distinct and clear sound.

Suddenly a sound came from somewhere, 'Don't throw that. That is very precious.'

With a sudden jerk, I looked in the direction of the sound. I found no one. I again looked at that stone. Since it was moonlight, so it is tough to ascertain what exactly it is.

Just then I recalled that I asked ketvig to take me to a place where there is no visible living creature. Is it again, some 'Pilly Pong' like creature? But if it would then also ketvig have found its biological signature. Then what it would be?

'Oh. Why am I not asking to ketvig', I thought.

'Ketvig, Is there any living organism?'

'No. There is no sign of any living organism,' replied ketvig.

'Then what it would be?,' I asked to myself.

I shouted and called many times, 'Hello....! Who is here? I will not harm you. I will be your friend. Come! Let's talk!'

Found no way out and after doing a lot of brainstorming, I concluded that the only way to find is to pretend again as if I am going to throw this stone.

So again, I walked near the lake and pretended as if I will throw it.

The same voice came but this time the sound is coming from somewhat a nearer place. I still was looking here and there in order to find, what actually is this, which is not being shown as a living being.

'I was wondering a lot.'

'Look! Look in this direction, you, sixteenth generation robot,' a feeble voice came from my left hand side.

Finding the voice coming closer to me. I, without any thought, as a reflex, hold that stone tightly in a way that if some mishappening will occur then I can throw it in order to protect myself.

# 14.

# I ... , A Robot?

When I saw the thing which was asking me not to throw that stone, I was jaw-struck and I calmed myself.

It was very adorable and cute, looking like a toy robot of size of about twenty centimeters long. I was very excited to hold it.

As soon as I extended my hand to hold it, it flew away. I ran behind it. I forget about everything that where am I, what am I doing, and what it said.

After hurtling helter-skelter behind it, when I got tired. Then it again said, be at ease you, sixteenth generation robot.

'Me. Robot!'

'No... I am not a robot. I am a human being,' I shouted in retaliation and tried to prove my point by saying, 'I am Hellry. I am twelve years old.'

That adorable robot tried to explain, 'Oh Hellry! Let me explain to you. We all are made up of the same elements. Some just evolved with time and became independent in many aspects like movement, energy transformation, communication, sensation, development, growth and reproduction.'

'Although everything in the universe is made up of about one hundred and eighteen elements, it is only their association and bonding which helps us evolve. And for bonding, they require perfect condition in the form of the environment which is provided mainly by Stars, which itself is made up of the simplest element- Hydrogen.'

'So, if you explore rationally then you will find that everything gets energy from the simplest element, as it forms the stars. And with that other elements come into existence. And when these elements join together, different compounds come into existence, having diverse physical and chemical properties.'

I was totally fixed in a fix, listening and thinking.

It continued, 'For the purpose of evolution, newer and complex molecules are required.'

‘First generation robots are landforms like mountains, rivers, lakes, etc, which are made up of very small and simple molecules like silica, water, and some other oxides, so they transform themselves very slowly.’

'I am a tenth-generation robot, named Smalli.

'From the outside, I am made up of simple molecules, but from inside I have some typical molecules which help me to store data, communicate and have sense.

Smalli added, 'Before me lies some single-celled organisms, and before them lies virus.'

'Wait... Wait,' I shouted in order to have some time as it was tough for me to put myself with non-living things. However, I was trying my best to understand things that Smalli explained to me.

Now that lake seems to me as if it is staring at me. And that silvery grass is basking in the moonlight. I don't know whether the stone that I pelted is happy or sad. Happy may be because of soaking in the lake and moving with the water. Sad may be because of being separated from fellow stones.

'Where have you lost yourself, sixteenth-generation robot?' asked Smalli.

'Please don't ... don't call me a robot. I am Hellry. And I am not lost... I am just thinking. Thinking about plants.’

‘Oh.. those eighteenth-generation robots.'

I could not stop myself and with a grin said, ‘Plant! Eighteenth generation! How?’

‘Plants are inferior to us. Even they developed before us. Not they?’

'Yes. They have developed before you on this planet. But they are superior to you in the most important facet that is energy transformation- they are independent. Their growth and survival never harm the environment. They support lives. Although they don't travel but their progeny can travel very far in the form of seed.'

'As far as you talk about age. Then be very clear, humans are aliens to this planet. That's why they do not understand and so respect other beings. Coming here they become lazy and over time, they forget about their origin.'

Everything was appearing ghostly and despite being a full moon night, now there was ghast darkness in front of my eyes.

‘So ...’

Smalli continued, 'You would be much surprised to know that humans are restricted from entering the fourth dimension, just in order to preserve this planet even when they have utilized all the resources and damaged much of flora and fauna alongwith other robots who are endemic to this planet.'

‘But ..' I recalled, 'Oh. I can come to this dimension because of k-way and survive here because of that dreaded chemistry lab incident.'

'Then why are you here? Because I think you are also not an inhabitant of this planet, Earth.'

‘Yes.’

'You are right. I came from robot planet itself, where new robots evolve and specimens of all old and developing robots are kept.'

'It is very ironic that in order to check evolution and bring monopoly, one of the generations of the robot has cut off the energy supply to the robot planet.'

'Therefore, we have been sent on a mission to find someone who can resume the energy supply and let the evolution continue in this universe in order to bring harmony and peace.'

'How evolution can bring harmony and peace.'

'Look for the plants. Do they fight? Do they harm other beings?'

'NO.. I think they never harm anyone, except some insectivorous plants.'

'Can you give a reason why insectivorous plants harm others?'

'That's very simple. Because they have to take essential minerals or nutrients that they don't get from surrounding or that they can't prepare.'

'It means you are saying that if one can get all the necessary minerals and can prepare different molecules necessary for their survival then they will not harm others.'

'Yes. Surely.'

'This is the secret of evolution. Evolution is always done with a purpose that is to bring harmony and peace.'

# 15.

# For The Sake Of Evolution

'Is empathy the key to evolution', I asked to myself.

In that vast space with silvery grass, a milky lake and soothing air, only we three are there. I, smalli and my companion, ketvig. Now everything assumes to me as living. The difference between living and non-living has waned.

Just then, I felt that a small finger-like thing was touching my cheek and is trying to turn my face towards the right-hand side and feebly uttered, 'See, those are Areola Borealis. Electromagnetic lights. They are the main source which results in evolution as they help in forming new chemicals. Newer chemicals have new properties. Those properties only allow for added and better features.'

'Can you tell me, Why sixteenth-generation robots fight among themselves?'

'What?'

'Oh! I mean, Why do Humans fight among themselves?'

I thought for a while and then said with my eyes narrowly opened, 'I guess, maybe because of overpopulation.'

'Yes! Don't hesitate! You are very correct.'

'Humans organized themselves and formed a union which they refer as caste, race or religion or regional. These groups try to prevent other groups from using limited resources, so they fight. And it is very ridiculous that for fighting they utilize that limited resources which they would have shared with others.'

'They have to take only one and very determined and holistic decision that to restrict population growth in all the places despite the population concentration in that region or locality.'

By that time, the moon is now moving towards horizons as a lot of time has passed and after some time twilight is going to happen.

Smalli somewhat louder than its usual tone asked, 'WAIT! How can you be here in this fourth dimension? This is not possible for humans to come here and survive here. So, how can you be?'

I briefly narrated my whole story.

'Oh then, you are perfect for me.'

'For what,' I enquired with much suspicion as everything happening is not only unusual but also very new to me, even newer than my thoughts and daydreams.

Smalli, instead of answering me, took out his left palm and with its right index finger pressed its left middle finger, and sooner its left palm started appearing like a small keyboard, just like the remote controller of a Television. But unlike that, it has some weird-looking buttons.

'Are you ready, sixteenth generation robot?'

'SORRY!'

'Are you ready, Hellry?'

I sternly and pressingly asked, 'FOR WHAT?'

'For resuming the energy supply of Robot planet! That's simple.'

'BUT HOW? That is very far from here. As you have told me. So how can we go there?'

I was astonishingly asking many questions. But despite paying any heed to me, Smalli was busy pressing keys in its left palm.

Smalli, while continuing pressing, peered towards me and with a robotic-fashioned smile, told enthusiastically, 'This communication device is gifted to me by a twenty-second generation robot. It can help me in calling them and informing them about my whereabouts.'

Meanwhile, I heard some whizzing sound which drew my attention towards itself and it was a very big, gigantic, and stupendous horse-like. NO! NO! it would be better to call like a unicorn because it has wing-like fins. And it was moving very fast towards us. I looked towards smalli.

Smalli was very content and was looking very happy and its robotic eyes are widely opened. And is seeming very excited to see that thing.

Before I could have said anything. Smalli patted on me on my shoulder and gestured to move forward toward the coming horse. Oh NO! Unicorn-like floating object.

Although Smalli has not told me anything but it is easy to understand that whoever will be in this or this, is known to Smalli. And must be harmless.

Coming nearer, that unicorn-like thing, is now visible to its fullest. Although dimly because it is still night. It is colossal. A faint light is coming out from the corners of that spaceship.

Before touching the ground, it bent its front leg and extended its rear leg so as to touch the ground first from its rear leg. Just after touching the ground, it leaned forward and pressed hard with its front leg and then stood upright.

It was very big, bigger than a truck.

After its landing, the head-like structure of that unicorn-like spaceship detached and landed gently on the ground. It was about the size of an SUV car.

Now the inner part becomes visible. It has a centre table with lots of switches and screens, surrounded by some chairs, which seem to be much adjustable. I guessed it probably because of the varied generation of robots that join this table.

A soft-toned voice came, 'Smalli! Come inside. And take Hellry with you. We have already wasted many years in finding anyone who has other power than the power given to them by the robotic planet during their evolution. And Hellry is only one among the whole universe.'

Smalli flew and traversing the car's roof went inside the car and sat on a chair after adjusting its height and size that would best fit Smalli.

Since it was tough for me to get there as I have to climb in order to reach inside. I tried my best to hold the corners to draw myself upward. But it was of no use. Then only, I felt that a chair is just behind me. And Smalli uttered, 'Come fast Hellry! Sit on that chair.'

Finding this, I just laughed at myself that why can't I would have understood that if they have such technology, then they must be having some technology for this also?

As I sat on that chair. The reverse started happening. Head attached. The front leg left the ground first. Followed by the rear leg. Then we were in the sky.

For some moment, I was totally blank. Maybe because of the unexpected that is happening or because of the underlying fear that what will happen next or due to the reason as I have not been informed about this at my home.

# 16.

# Journey Beyond

I don't know how long it took. Because there was only black colour surrounding me as if it was night.

Since I was having a lot of questions which I think Smalli can answer. So, I thought to ask these questions from it.

I asked, 'Why everyone speaks only one language?'

'It's very simple. As they all have evolved from the same place.'

'Then, why on the Earth, every species, even humans of different regions have a different language.'

'First thing first. On Earth, different species use different languages as they tried to diversify themselves in a group. But one species of any place has the same language.'

'As for the Humans, the reason is the same. But it wanted to further group themselves according to region, religion, etc, so they differentiated their language in order to keep privacy and communicate only with their alikes even when they are surrounded by different groups.'

I was totally amazed by this answer. My eyes opened wide. I was in a state of shock. Is this really the reason behind the enormous language and cultural diversity? It seems somewhat correct to me when I reason in myself that we all humans do our basic daily activities, in the same way, irrespective of knowledge, living standard, economic status, region, or religion.

With the sudden gong, which might be because of some asteroid hitting the metallic ship, I guessed that we might be passing through the asteroid belt. I looked towards my ketvig. It was blank.

I can understand that grandpa has not assumed that his invented ketvig will go to space. And that too sooo.. far.

'Oh no! I have missed my laserboard,' I mumbled.

Smalli interrupted, 'We are about to reach.'

Hellry was taken aback as he was thinking that he might be passing the asteroid belt but he has passed not only the asteroid belt but also the Kuiper belt alongwith the solar system and the milky way galaxy. And would have travelled many Astronomical Units, a unit used in space exploration. One Astronomical Unit is equal to the distance between the Sun and the Earth's orbit.

Hellry looking here and there in order to find any meter or device which would state speed like an odometer in our cars. Not finding anything similar. Hellry in a perplexed fashion asked Smalli, 'With what speed we have travelled?'

Smalli trying to be very content but could not control itself and with a feeble smile answered, 'You would be surprised to know that it is only a sixteenth-generation robot, I mean Humans, who have invented a way to move through portals. And by that system, they moved to the Earth and started exploiting that planet. With time they become so lazy and unaware that they themselves forget about their technology.

'So, I have just used their technology. And travelled afar within minutes.'

'Then what was that gong.'

'Oh! That metallic gong. It was nothing. It was just a notification to state that we are out of the portal.'

'Now we have to close this question-answer round,' Smalli said with a wide robotic smile and wide robotic eye.

Suddenly Smalli changed its look and started looking serious, with a narrow eye.

'LOOK! Now you have to be very cautious. Since we don't know which generation of robots have turned it off and what was their motive behind doing that.'

'But,' Hellry yelled, 'You told me that they have done this to stop evolution.'

'We guessed that this might be the reason. But we are not sure as we even don't know, who has turned it off.'

'BE FOCUSSED!' Smalli hissed.

Meanwhile, the SUV-like head of that unicorn-like ship detached and landed swiftly. Before I could have spoken anything, my chair started flying following Smalli. We reached beside a large rock. There the chair landed and relieved me from its clutches and returned back. Smalli approached me and asked feebly that we have to wait here for a moment unless I receive a sign to proceed.

'Who will give you this message.'

'Shhh! Please be quiet!'

Finding the free time, I started gazing at the surrounding. It was almost like our Earth. The place where we were hiding is almost surrounded by hills from three sides. It was high. Almost as high as six floors. It was startling.

'I and this sixteenth-generation robot want to reboot the system. So please allow us to get in.'

When I heard this sentence then I looked to my left from where these words were being uttered. It was Smalli mumbling very close to this rock.

'Smalli! This is a rock. It has no ears, even if it is living,' I asked Smalli in an informing way.

'Hellry, why don't you try to speak near your skin?'

I tried. It really works.

'Hellry, amongst the five sense organs you humans have, the largest one is skin. From which you perceive temperature and pressure. And since speech is a sound wave and its warmness adds emotions. So even speech can be perceived by skin, although very faintly.'

Till then, that rock moved aside. And the place from where it moved has a tunnel-like depression. Smalli moved inside. So, I followed it. Inside was a huge hall with lots of pictures drawn on the wall alongwith texts.

'Is this a museum?'

Smalli faintly answered as if it does not want to let anyone know about their presence, 'Yes! It is a museum where the details of all the robots are kept as well as the serious flaws that they have or why they were developed further are also mentioned here.'

We heard some footsteps. Smalli and I both were terrified as here, there is almost nothing to hide. Although Smalli is very small, but it was tough for me to hide. Finding this, we both looked at each other. Both have no answer or suggestion. Footsteps become clearer and louder suggesting that it is coming nearer to us.

Smalli hinted to me to sit in the corner where there is somewhat dim light. And it asked me to be silent and breathe softly. So I sat in the corner facing the wall. And it came near my shoulder and tried to hide itself. As the footsteps were becoming louder, we both were getting very nervous and our pulses is increasing.

'There it is', a coarse voice with a sharp tone directed others.

These words shook both of us from our core. It was like our end is destined. We both were chilled. And cold sweats appeared on my forehead. This is for the first time when I am so much frightened. I felt as if I am solitary standing in a very vast field with a white atmosphere and dark sporadic clouds. I forget about Smalli.

'Yes! There it is. Come fast. Let's have a look.' Another voice followed the first one. It was very serious and coarse. The tone of the voice was suggesting that they were very tall and have strong built and are merciless.

Although I was very frightened and was shrinking as if I should become as small as I can, I tried to feel for Smalli.

Smalli is not by my side.

Finding Smalli not by my side has just drawn-out soul from my body. I felt as if I will collapse. I was in a state of shock. I have regrets about coming here. About trusting Smalli.

A sudden but gentle blow on my arm took out my breath. I closed my eyes tightly.

'Hellry, Wake up! How can you sleep here?'

'What!' I exclaimed in myself and tried to figure out who can it be. Only one answer was there. It can be no other than Smalli. Although it was embarrassing that it is thinking that I was sleeping. But finding Smalli has not only allayed my fear but also emboldened me. Because if it is speaking so confidently then they must be known to Smalli. And there is no danger. I guessed.

'They want to meet you.'

'Who are they?'

'Oh! Of course. I forget to introduce them to you.'

'Look in that side.'

Hellry looked in a specific direction where they were gazing at a piece of the mural. They were three- one, like a small bubble, another like a giant beast, and the third one is like a big spider.

'Of those three- that small bubble-like is the twenty-second generation robot. It can merge with the environment. It is the most advanced.'

Hellry recalled and surmised that it must be a species of Pilly-Pong.

'That giant beast is a fifteenth-generation robot. And the third one is a nineteenth-generation robot.'

'What they are doing there?' Hellry inquired in amusement.

'There they were trying to know about sixteenth-generation robots that are humans as they want to know about you before meeting you so that they can greet you in your way.'

I thought, 'This is really very interesting.'

'What is this?' I questioned myself as on the floor there starts appearing s small circle of white colour whose circumference was increasing in size and also its colour started changing from white to BYR (Blue - Yellow - Red ). The three primary colours. It was stupendous. Later on, that too starts splitting into GOV (Green - Orange - Violet). The three secondary colours. My eyes were fixed. It was appearing as if the smoke of colours is dispersing and changing its forms. Although it was fast. But it startled me.

The magic was about to end. I was content. Then soon one more colour appeared between Violet and Blue, that is Indigo.

Followed by this, everything started changing and, in a moment, the circumferential spread of colours arranged themselves and formed a Rainbow (VIBGYOR). And the 'WELCOME' word appeared diametrically.

Really it was a warm welcome. I was impressed. Feeling high.

When I came back to my senses then I felt that I am surrounded by others. Only the twenty-second generation robot, the Pilly-Pong species, was missing.

I guessed that this colourful welcome must be done by Pilly-Pong as I have seen it earlier also. They are really magnificent.

Smalli announced, 'Listen! Back to work. Here we are on a very important mission. So, please share your ideas and intuition. As we have to plan things based on both because we don't have any data or relevant information.

With this announcement, everyone arranged themselves in a circle. And sooner the floor started rising and took a shape of a circular table. And rest took the shape of chairs.

'Don't be amazed,' a growling voice by a fifteenth-generation robot, 'These floors are made up of elastic material like your muscles. It flexes itself and took the desired shape when required. And since they have senses, so they feel your requirement and act accordingly like your pets.'

# 17.

# Executing Plan

Nineteenth-generation robot clearing its throat said, 'What I feel that this must be done with a purpose to hinder evolution.'

'Not hinder. But to stop evolution', the fifteenth-generation robot in its coarse voice sternly espoused, 'We must do something very fast to stop the evolving species and others whose life is directly supported by the functioning of the evolutionary machine, as they might suffocate and die or have already died.'

'WHAT! Will they really die?,' Hellry jumped from his chair while asking this. As death means a lot to him. He knows what others feel when you die, as he has witnessed it after his chemistry lab incident. And he also knows what one feels when death is about to ensue as he has witnessed it right now when he heard the footsteps.

Hellry certainly knows the value of life. And why not. One must know its value and regard it by abstaining from doing those things where life comes in danger.

'Why are we wasting time and why was those colourful welcome? We are costing many lives. Be fast. Tell me what to do,' Hellry continued and told everything in a single breath. Gasping heavily.

'Okay!', Smalli interrupted, 'What you have to do is this to go in the funnelled corner of the hall that you will find after a maze. Where you have to solve some riddles to find your way. And after the narrow corridor, you will find that hall.'

'No one can give you company in this ordeal as that passage was designed in such a fashion that no one can survive who has a simple evolutionary lineage.'

Speaking coarsely but gently and expressing its insufficiency, the fifteenth-generation robot added, 'It is only you who have powers other than those given by evolutionary planet. So only you can go there with our best wishes.'

'I hope you would be ready and prepared for this ordeal', the Pilly-Pong-like species enquired.

'Yes! I am.'

Everyone waved Hellry. However, he was a bit hesitant but full of zeal as he is determined enough to save lives, for which he is now fully aware that he can't waste time gathering information that can help him in accomplishing his task more comfortably and easily.

So, he ran towards one of the gates of the hall which everyone has directed as the entrance of that maze.

As Hellry entered the maze he was mesmerized by its beauty, it has no riddles instead it has very attractive colour signage which is directing the way. Hellry followed it but sooner he guessed some foul play as things can't be so easy. As soon as he expressed distrust, all the colours started changing and the pleasing colour and the soothing ambiance were now appearing to be very dark and bad odour with dark smoke started accumulating in that maze.

These perturbed Hellry a lot and for a while, he forgets about the lives of those whose fate lies in the hands of Hellry. Again, he tried to control himself and remembered the words of his grandpa, 'BE EMPATHETIC!'

This brought a fresh strength in him, which in turn gave him not only hope but also trust in his surrounding that they will certainly help him in saving lives. As he freshened himself with a fresh lease of hope and trust, reverse ensued and again the ambiance become soothing and magnificent. Again, signage appeared.

This, all, emboldened Hellry that if someone is doing good to you or something is happening which is considered good, then it is not always that you are going to be deceived or you are lured. Have faith. Positive faith. Atleast there it seems the norm.

He, now, followed the signage and reached the narrow corridor. In that corridor, what he saw left him shocked as after a distance of only four feet there is a door on which a painting is made which changes with every step. And as Hellry reached near the door and pushed it in order to open it. The question appeared on the door.

It was not tough for Hellry to understand that this question is based on the picture that he saw on the door. As Hellry has not watched those pictures nicely so Hellry moved back guessing that those pictures will reappear. But to his despair, pictures do not reappear. Even questions started fainting.

Finding no other option, Hellry moved forward near the door. Read the question. Focussed. And closed his eyes tightly. Looked upward. Struck his forehead gently with his index finger and took a deep breath. Recalled everything starting from entering the maze. Soon he found himself in a state of calmness.

'YES! I recalled,' Hellry said gently but with much excitement and zest.

Punched the answer. And as anyone can guess. Door opened. Hellry excitedly was about to move forward. Again, he was taken aback when he found that there is no floor in the consequent corridor.

Hellry in desperation kicked the door and felt very heavy-hearted as someone will cost their life because of this delay. What he can do?

Hellry was passing through a very tough time. Whether he should return back to take the help of his multi-talented new friends or wait for some new miracle to happen. He soon realized that both can't be done as his friends can't come here and it is useless to wait for miracles to happen. Then What?

'Think Hellry! THINK!'

'Why not open this door and use it as a platform,' he questioned himself.

Soon he started to find ways to open it and to his surprise, the pictures and questions asked by that door have an answer in themselves. He closed back the door. Cut the hinge of the door. Locked the bottom rail of the door with the anchorage on the floor near the saddle (threshold). Pushed the door towards the ground. A little space started appearing between the top rail of the door and the upper casing of the door.

'Now, time to push,' he asked to himself. And besides pushing it from the side, Hellry pushed it from the top. The door fell down and covered that gap.

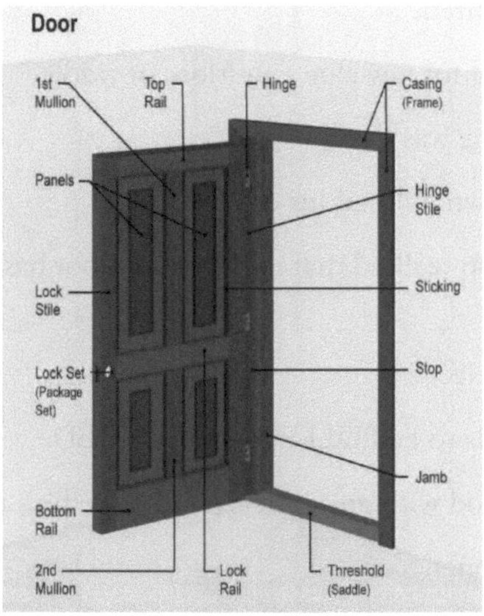


Although Hellry wants to be content but it was tough for him to be content in achieving such a feat.

He moved forward but with caution as he was expecting a question followed by some pictures. Nothing happened like that. He was preparing himself for any other kind of challenge. No change. Everything normal.

'Okay then. Let me push it.'

He closed his eyes and pushed the door awaiting some new surprises.

He was surprised not because there was anything unusual but because the door was not opened by pushing.

He pushed it harder.

But of no use.

Tried again.

Lastly tired.

Looked for any clue, question, or riddle.

Nothing was there.

Sat down. Closed his eyes.

He soon realized that the previous door has no handle but it has.

'MEANS'

It needs to be PULLED, not PUSHED.

He stood with great energy and pulled it.

Door opened.

Now it was the hall with different-looking machines and things.

He entered very cautiously and based on his previous experiences, he is now focused and trying to examine everything with sharp eyes. It was just like clicking photographs of everything.

He found the funnelled corner of the hall. He reached there slowly.

What to do here. As no one guided him.

He forgot to ask.

'No. Actually, I heard that coarse voice who was asking me to stop and listen first.'

But I was in such a haste to save lives that now it will pay.

'Since it is not possible to return back, it is better to examine what can be done to resume this robot planet.'

Hellry one by one examined all the nooks, corners, and crevices alongwith bigger places. He found no switches, no plugs, no sockets, or any wires that can be connected. Literally saying there was nothing like wires. Everything seems to conduct anything when required. This means the same thing is both insulators and conductors. It depends on the requirement.

By this time, Hellry has learned that recalling things by closing the eyes and controlling the mind from moving here and there is the best way to find a solution than questioning and reasoning. So, he closed his eyes, tried to meditate, and recall the things from where the things started happening, means from the lakeside.

Recalling the silvery-grass and milky-lake gave him immense pleasure and a serene smile appeared. Then that stone-pelting incident.

'Oh! It's in my bag.'

He opened his favourite self-styled, self-sewn purple bag. Delved into it. The feeble smile cropped up which is a clear indication that he found that which he is looking for. Without any delay, he took out that biscuit-like stone. It is for the first time that he looked at it clearly as before this he only felt its texture because it was dark. It has many grooves and crevices like an ancient artifact. Have colourful gems embedded on its periphery and a rhombus-shaped very brilliant coloured hemispheric gem is in the center.

As soon as he took it out, and put it in his palm in order to have a look at it. Different rays emerged from those gems and after travelling for some distance, they took a curvilinear path. And passed through all the obstacles. It seems that it wants to reach somewhere. 'BUT WHERE?'

Hellry followed it with that stone in its palm. He found that rays of light are entering some grooves. On examining it with sharp eyes, he established that it is the opposite design of this stone. BINGO! It means that this must fit into this.

Although now it is sure that it will fit into the specific place, Hellry got terrified as there is nothing usual. As he recollected the light ray always follows a rectilinear path but here it is travelling in a curvilinear fashion. These rays are like magnets getting drawn toward a specific place. How do laws of physics not hold here? What may happen if I put this stone in its specified place? Will some unusual events ensue putting me and others in danger?

‘I have no time to reason these. Anyhow, I have to save lives,’ he emboldened himself and tried to bolster his confidence.

Hellry gathering all his energies and confidence closed his breath for a while and inserted the stone in its specified groove.

NOTHING HAPPENED!

Hellry was a bit confused. Whether he has placed it incorrectly or in the wrong place.

‘No, it can’t be,’ he reasoned in himself, ‘as the colour emerging from the gems has been correctly matched to those places where it was entering.’

‘There must be any password or voice activation system or anything related.’

Hellry was busy exploring the ways to activate it or reasoning in himself that he missed anything, etc.

Meanwhile, the roof of that hall silently opened, which was not noticed by Hellry until he heard the snapping sound which happened when the joints come to halt. He looked upward. Taken aback. As the whole sky is clear to him. It was marvellous.

‘Wow! It’s very wonderful.’

Before he could have exclaimed it properly. He moved that floor is moving. He trembled. Tried to balance himself and understand what is happening. Finding no answer, he ran helter-skelter towards the door from where he came inside. When he reached near the door, he moved further to open it.

'THUD!'

His head bumped into an obstacle. It was transparent like glass. But very clear. Clear enough to get confused that anything is there. He tried to feel it with his hand. When he touched it with his hand and moved it in order to find any gap or anything. Again to his disappointment, he found nothing useful. He was feeling gloomy so he want to return back to that place where he has inserted that stone.

Again, 'THUD!'

'What's this!' Hellry questioned, 'I can't move further. Even the things disappeared from my sight.'

He understood that he was in a glass-like cage. For him, things are becoming bleak. He can now understand that how Fastest Leg has felt. When he remembered of Fastest Leg, a very different sort of energy channelized in him, boosting him to try further. He, again, tried to explore that glass-like periphery.

At a place, he felt, that something happened. He moved back. And placed his hand very cautiously.

'Welcome Hellry! Thanks for your help in rebooting the robot planet!' a computerized IVR-like sound told, 'For this journey, I am your personal guide.'

Hellry interrupted and loosing his patience asked, 'JOURNEY! Where am I going? What is this? And what happened to persons- are they alright?'

'This ship is going to drop you on your planet Earth.'

'And I am sorry to inform you that about one thousand thirty-nine robots lost their lives because of this.'

'Here, you have a gift from Smalli, as it was not able to show itself to you and say you bye-bye, as per the guidelines of this planet. Open that box placed in the corner.'

Hellry found that box. Opened it. There were two things- the first one, is familiar to Hellry, a headphone and the other one is, a pouch. He put that headphone on his head and was trying to find his audio device from his bag to connect it. But before he could have done it, he heard the voice of Smalli, 'Thanks Hellry! On behalf of the robotic planet and the Universe. As your deed was very important for letting the evolution continue and for the fate of this vast Universe. I am sorry that I have not come to see you off personally because of the decorum of this robotic planet. And the demise of many robots. Oh! In the next pouch, I.. not we have given you a small gift but it is of much use. It is an Atomter.'

Hellry anxiously opened that pouch, it has a similar stone that he had just now placed to reboot the robot planet.

The voice continued, 'Everything in this universe is made up of elements, that too counted elements, about 118. And the smallest part of that element is called an atom. But all atoms are made up of common things- electrons, protons, and neutrons. It is their numbers which make an atom characteristic of other. This atomter is a device which if properly calibrated then can change the number of electrons, protons, or neurons or any two or all three. Thus, helps in converting atoms of one kind to other. This is the answer to why even the Sun can be immortal.'

‘Please accept it and take a rest. In a few hours, you will pass through the portal and travel a very long distance in minutes.’

Yeah! I really need sleep or not sleep than a power-nap because I am both physically and mentally tired. I sat in a corner and gazed at the sky for a moment then closed my eyes.

# 18.

# Conundrum

'Boom!'

'The heart has been destroyed,' said one of the soldiers.

Captain yelled, 'we still have one more.'

With a roaring war cry, all the soldiers as well as the captain filled themselves with new zeal and zest. And approached further.

The sky is filling with smoke and dust. The odour is very heady. This makes a clear sense that the war not only destroys peace but also perturbs the interwoven fabric of nature with humans- both parties of war. The smoke is so dense that even the Sun is not clearly visible. The civilians are bearing the burnt of all these. They are in complete despair as the hope is becoming bleak and bleak with the passage of each and every day. Although they have become habituated to all this. But their daily lives, education, and development of children are severly affected. And a constant fear of new surprises tears apart their confidence and rob smiles from their face.

'Let's go!' Captain ordered with much confidence although her face was becoming white and her lips were dry, even after continuous licking of her lips. This is a sign of dehydration. But in a bid to achieve her goal, she is neither thinking of her body's demand nor she is paying heed to her wounds.

'But, how can we go there,' asked one of the soldiers, 'mam, there is very tight security. Going there will be just like committing suicide.'

'We must work out some plan,' the captain said and thought for a while and then asked with new hope, 'call the cartographer and technician. Be fast! As we all losing time.'

Within a minute, all the technicians from different fields and the team of cartographers reported.

'Yes, Mam! We are at service.'

'Relax!'

'Can you show me the map where your intel suggests that the heart is kept.'

'Although there is a different notion. But our four different teams have confirmed that the heart has been kept in the chamber next to the chamber of dragons. As it is the dragon that can sense and smell humans and become active and ferocious. And they are very loyal to their masters. And the chamber is at the tip of the tower.'

'So, it is very easy. We can approach there with our air support. And we have to destroy it only. Which we can do by holistically bombing the tower.'

'No mam!' interrupted one of the technicians.

Correcting himself and improving himself, cleared his throat and said in a well-mannered way, 'Sorry mam. But, I beg to differ with you, we can't bomb it to dust as in order to avoid this from happening they are running one preschool on the ground floor and one old-age home on the fourth floor.'

'Oh! Taking refuge of children and old. Such a coward act.'

'So, what can be done?'

All were silent. Everyone is looking at the map and other details very keenly. Some are discussing some plans or ways with some selected one or the one who can provide support-either information or possibility.

Meanwhile, the captain is working out some calculations and she shows the results to one of the technicians. That technician calibrated that equation into the 3D graph.

'Bingo! It can work.'

All looked excitedly and with anticipation toward that technician. For a moment, he sighed and gently pointed through his eyes toward the captain.

'Okay! Let me explain. As we all know that going from the ground is like committing suicide. And targeting hearts from the air is also difficult because of those dragons who can smell human flesh from very far. And we can't bomb the whole building as it houses a school and old-age home'

'So the plan is- I am making three teams. One will climb from outside the building. The second team will be carried by air who will paraglide. And the third team will also be carried by air but at two minutes apart, who is supposed to destroy that heart, which if not destroyed give them immense power.'

'Please don't mind, madam! But you have not explained the role of the first team.'

'First team! The first team is the support team. Who will carry out the work if the second team anyhow not able to reach at a destined place or on time.'

Their movement will follow the laws of physics-Mechanics. As the success only depends on the Time-Distance graph. If we miss this. We will certainly fail.

'The second time who is paragliding and two minutes ago has the only work to attract those ruthless dragons towards them. And in order to protect themselves, they have to fly at a faster pace than them. After carrying for about twenty minutes, these paragliders will directly land in the bunkers. So that they should not be hurt by those dragons. Disheartened dragons will take another twenty minutes to travel back.'

'So, the third team will have forty minutes to destroy that heart and get back,' exclaimed one soldier.

The captain continued, 'Meanwhile the first team will reach the top of the tower and wait for any message from the second team or central command.'

'Is that clear to everyone- soldiers, technicians and analysts,' asked the captain with a loud and attentive voice.

All replied together and with full of energy and hope, 'No, Mam!'

By the dawn, everyone prepared themselves both logistically and mathematically. Now it's time to act. The Ground team departed with much vigour. Paragliders took help from the big logistic airplane. And the destroyers moved by helicopter.

As the paragliders jumped off the airplane, the dragons sniffed and made loud noises then flew in the sky in the direction of the paragliders. All the paragliders shivered, seeing the dragons coming in their direction. But soon they realized that the analysts have made all the calculations very correctly as they were not able to reach near them. It seems that the relative velocity of dragons and paragliders is zero as both were maintaining a constant distance.

Followed by paragliders, destroyers took the help of ropes and reached the peak of the tower. Now it's time to find that dreaded heart. They pressed their watch which started showing them a 3D map of that place. They communicated with the base camp. Now base camp. Put them live on that 3D map. And give them direction which will lead them to heart. They have in total of thirty-eight minutes. Of that, they have passed six minutes. And they have to leave the building five minutes before the expected arrival of the dragons so that dragons can't see destroyers and follow them. Therefore, we have only twenty-one minutes to accomplish this mission and return safely, announced the team leader.

'Hurry up!'

After about nine minutes, they reached the right place. And seen that dire heart. They took the base team on a live feed. All were very happy finding that the team has reached safely and is about to destroy that heart.

Team-leader took out the necessary armamentarium and is about to destroy that heart.

Suddenly one of the team-member interrupted, 'Wait! This is a heart.'

Others looked towards her and someone asked, 'Then What! We are here to destroy it. Don't you know?'

Meanwhile, from the base camp, the captain asked, 'Who is she?'

'No! I mean Yes. I know that that we are here to destroy the heart. But the real one. Not the counterfeit one.'

'What do you mean?'

'Look at this heart. This is forged. This has no sheen as we were told during our training.'

'Alpha! Put the spectroscope near that heart. And be careful!'

One member came forward and took out the spectroscope and put it near the heart and connected the device to the base.

'Ah! She is right. This is not a real one.' asked the technician with distress and discomfort, scratching his head and taking out his glasses, 'what to do next?'

Just then, the radio set announced, 'We have landed safely in the bunkers.'

It means, now this team has only nine minutes to evacuate this place. And from the place where they have landed to this place, they took nine minutes.

Seeing the plan failing, the captain leaned on the monitor desk. And sighed heavily in great discomfort. Closed her eyes tightly. And annoyingly ordered, 'Destroyers evacuate! As fast as you can. Move to safety!'

Thought for a while and turned around, clenching her teeth, and asked, 'Delta! Execute the emergency plan! Confirmed! Note it! Emergency plan confirmed.'

Listening to this, adrenaline rushed into the veins of team members of destroyers and grounders. Grounders started putting bombs here and there on the outside of the building and triggering it. And rushing very fast to evacuate that building in order to take a safe passage.

While Destroyers are putting bombs at the pre-decided place that too very minutely in order to have maximum effect on the explosion of the bomb. While they are also considering the safe retreat as it is not only that they are concerned about their safety, but it is mainly because of the smelling capacity of the dragons. Who if sniff bomb then has a special power to detonate it. So, it is very necessary to retreat before their arrival.

The alarm system announced, only seven minutes left, of that, your effective time to evacuate the tower is, now, fifty-two seconds.

'Delta and others, be fast. We are too far.'

'Few more seconds I need.'

'Thirty'

'Fast!'

Everyone ran as fast as they can and tried to reach the terrace.

Two of the five members reached the terrace and the helicopter started rescuing them. All were in hurry. And everyone working with their full energy.

Among three, Delta and Alpha alongwith the team leader were left.

'Nineteen'

'Done, Sir! Let's retreat!'

All started running helter-skelter.

'Seven'

Moving very fast. Not even giving them enough time to catch their breath.

Escaping steps of the stairs. Alpha left her backpack in order to run faster. Delta also threw up the left bombs as well as his backpack.

'Three'

All reached the terrace and wanted to atleast take a deep breath. But have no time. Ran straight towards the rope.

'Rescuers move!' announced the radio set of helicopters.

'But! Mam! We still have three members to come.'

'We can't cost others for them. Move on!'

'Minus two'

'Alpha! Delta! Hop the rope!'

'Sir, you also!'

'Minus five'

A sudden smile appeared not only on the face of all five. But, also, on the face of the pilots of the helicopter. They turned back in order to congratulate them. And in retaliation, all members shook their heads as if they want to heartily thank them to saving their lives at the cost of their own lives. The short-lived melodrama ended with the sudden noise and smoke that filled the air and shooked even the helicopter. It was more violent than expected. Probably because of two reasons- one, maybe because of putting bombs in an unplanned manner by the ground team. Second, may be due to leaving behind the bombs by Delta.

Everyone was very happy. Even the base camp congratulated everyone and each member. This is the most significant moment for the captain and her team.

On the other side, the dragons have almost reached the tower but were not able to sniff the bomb or humans. They have failed. Now their shelter is gone. They are homeless.

Hidden somewhere in those smoke and rubbles are the cries and footsteps and shouting of old people and children.

This is a perturbing sight.

'NO! NO!' gasping heavily and moving his legs and arms, Hellry hit the glass-like panels of his spaceship.

As soon as he got hurt by the panels, he woke up. But still yet gasping. Tried to catch up his breath.

Soon he realized, it was a dream. A bad dream. He put his palm on his forehead to calm himself. But still, the sight of children and old people is in front of his eyes.

He developed sympathy for them. But only for them, but also for those robots who lost their lives on the robot planet. And, also, for them who Hellry don't know but are having pain and grief.

Hellry felt restless. Restless than before. It was getting very tough for him to find a way to solve all these types of problems.

He asked himself with a lot of stress and seriousness, 'How can I be more powerful?'

Asking this he moved his hand on the floor. He touched a pouch. It was the same pouch given by Smalli. He recalled it has the stone, Atomter. The one which can change the elements. The one which can even make the stars immortal. Very powerful. As only by harnessing and transforming energy, I can do this much. So, what if! What if, if I can be able to transform elements?

Hellry grinned.

But again, in the next moment, he becomes serious, thinking that how to use it.

He thought, 'Might be like the chemistry lab incident. As there the explosion gave me the power, here it might be possible, that breaking it will add power to me.

He prepared himself. As he has to do something for them-for the helpless. For this, he can go to any extent.

Took a deep breath. Closed his eyes. Jogged. And finally took the stone between his two hands and put extreme pressure on it. But nothing happened.

He put that stone on the floor and looked here and there. Found one hammer. Grabbed it and aimed it at the stone. And smashed it.

Beautiful colours of light emerged from it and filled the space. Then all the colours started shrinking. And in another moment, all the colours retreated. But the space has very soothing vibes. It was neither cold nor warm, neither light nor dark. It was something which have no words. For a moment, it all appeared very pleasing but brought no change. Hellry thought that nothing will happen. And he was also upset that he has damaged it. Whether it will work in the future or not.

Suddenly, the light reappeared traversed Hellry, and then filled all the space. It seems that Hellry became unconscious and the rays of light raised him from the floor. The rays go on increasing in number. And the colours which were initially stable started flickering. Something very unusual was happening. It seems that light is filling the spaceship. Every nook and corner. Every millimeter.

And suddenly spaceship exploded in pieces, it seems that the spaceship was not able to bear the pressure of those emitting lights. After all, it is an Atomter.

There was light everywhere. Like the Sun. But it was not warm. Slowly light started shrinking. Shrinking to a point. A center. Now nowhere is stone. Only a point. Small point.

That point started moving. Moved towards a floating body. Integrated as human. It was no other than Hellry.

But calm and composed. Silent and in peace. Eyes closed. A body floating in space. Like a leaf in the pond. Moving with waves. Sometimes slowly. Sometimes fastly. Sometimes at the same place. Sometimes to afar. These waves are not like water waves which can be felt. It is invisible.

# About The Author

Akshat Sreshtin was born in Nalanda, Bihar (India) on 30th September, 2011.

He began writing poems and short stories in 2021. He is a boarder at Manjusri Public School, Sikkim and presently studying in class VII.

He along with writing, enjoys painting and making scratch (***tigerofgreat***) on different issues and games since 2020.

Presently he is also trying to make animation and 3D Models using Blender for which he is also learning skills in Python and Microbit.

9 789358 194807

Printed by Libri Plureos GmbH in Hamburg, Germany